Lizzie McGuire
SUPER SPECIAL

A Totally Hottie Summer

DISCARDED

By Samantha Maridan

Based on the television series, "Lizzie McGuire", created by Terri Minsky

Disney PRESS

New York

CHAPTER ONE

"**S**o what kinds of things do you two kids want to do this summer?" Mrs. McGuire asked her children. She took a bite of the tofu-surprise casserole she had made for dinner that night, then smiled encouragingly at Lizzie and her ten-year-old brother, Matt. "After all," Mrs. McGuire added, "school will be over in two weeks."

Lizzie and Matt exchanged a look. Lizzie had no plans.

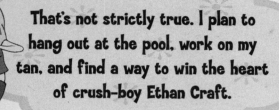

That's not strictly true. I plan to hang out at the pool, work on my tan, and find a way to win the heart of crush-boy Ethan Craft.

"Yes, Lizzie." Her father sounded interested. "Tell us what you've got planned."

Lizzie took a deep breath. "Well, I plan to . . . relax," she said truthfully. "I mean, I've been studying hard all year, and my brain needs a rest."

"What about you, Matt?" their dad asked.

The little rodent's grin widened. "I've been thinking about—music," he announced. "But I need to narrow it down. Right now, I'm not sure if I want work with a small ensemble, or maybe surf sounds or cutting-edge electronica."

"What do you know about surf sounds or electronica?" Lizzie asked.

"Lizzie." Her mom's voice had a warning tone in it. "I think you should stop questioning your brother's plans and make some of your own. Actually, I have the perfect idea."

Hmm—the perfect idea. Always a bad sign.

"What?" Lizzie asked warily.

"Volunteer work!" Mrs. McGuire proclaimed.

Lizzie looked at her mother in disbelief. "As in, I work all summer and don't earn a cent?"

"Well, you weren't exactly going to make big bucks with your relaxation plan," her dad pointed out.

"Lizzie, this is a wonderful opportunity,"

her mom said. "You're still young enough not to have to pay rent or buy your own gas. You have the freedom now to give your time and help others. You can make a real difference in someone else's life."

I've been ambushed! How can I possibly argue with that?

"It's not that I don't want to help others," Lizzie explained. "It's just that if I have to work all summer, it would be nice to earn something. I mean, you're always telling me that this family is on a budget, and there isn't enough money for all the clothes I want.

"You wouldn't earn that much, though," her dad pointed out. "Most summer jobs don't pay well."

Mrs. McGuire adjusted her black-rimmed glasses. "However, if you do volunteer this summer, we might be willing to increase your allowance a little. Just to be fair."

"Really?" That part didn't sound so bad.

Her mother nodded. "I just happen to have a list of organizations that need volunteers. You'll need to move quickly, sweetie. These positions fill up fast." Mrs. McGuire handed Lizzie an eight-page, single-spaced list. "I've even given you the Web site for each group, so you can fill out online applications."

Lizzie knew there was no way she'd ever get out of this one. "Great," she said, taking the list and forcing a smile. "Thanks, Mom."

"You'll see, honey. It's the volunteers who really benefit," Mrs. McGuire told her. "They always get so much more than they put in. When you volunteer for a good cause, you're the one who winds up feeling good."

I already know what makes me feel good—swimming and shopping!

* * *

"Are your parents asking you to make summer plans?" Lizzie asked Miranda Sanchez and David "Gordo" Gordon. It was a Friday evening, and Lizzie had invited her two best friends over for a strategy session. Maybe together, they could figure out a cool summer plan.

"Not really. I'm pretty much set," Gordo admitted.

"Me, too," Miranda said.

"You both have plans and didn't tell me?" Lizzie asked indignantly.

Miranda shrugged. "It was no big deal. Last night, my aunt Alejandra asked me to work in her new restaurant three days a week. It doesn't pay much, but it's something. So I said yes."

"And last month I applied for one of those internships at the *Hillridge Daily Chronicle*," Gordo began. "You know how it works. Every summer, they choose a group of interns from the local junior highs to put together the Youth Page. There are only five positions and dozens of applicants." He shrugged. "I never really thought I'd get picked."

Lizzie sighed and sank down onto her bed. "Congratulations, Gordo. That's really great," she said. "And, Miranda, your job sounds cool, too. But what am *I* going to do?"

Gordo glanced at Mrs. McGuire's eight-page list. "You could volunteer for something," he suggested. "It might not be so bad."

Lizzie shook her head stubbornly. "I went

through that list. I didn't see anything that I want to do."

"Well, what *do* you want to do?" Miranda asked her.

"Yeah." Gordo was getting into it now. "We should make a list of your priorities and use that to match you up with a volunteer slot." He slid over to her computer. "May I?" he asked, his hands hovering over her keyboard.

"Go to it," Lizzie said.

Gordo called up a blank page and typed: *Lizzie's Priorities.* "What are they?" he asked.

Lizzie shut her eyes and imagined her dream summer job.

Costarring in a movie with Ethan Craft! With lots of kissing scenes!

She opened her eyes with a giggle. "Being near lots of hotties," she said. "Working with Ethan would be perfecto, but I'll also consider other awesome cute guys."

"That figures." Gordo typed: *1. Proximity to Hotties (E. Craft preferred).*

Lizzie glanced at the screen and winced. "That sounds so shallow."

"Ya think?" Gordo asked, smiling.

"I also want a job that's interesting," Lizzie said, "one where I don't have to do the exact same thing day after day."

"Good," Gordo said, and typed: *2. Interesting work, variety.*

"I want to meet interesting people, maybe even make new friends," Lizzie added. "And, I want to be able to wear stylin' clothes, not some dopey uniform."

Gordo added: *3. Interesting peers. 4. Decent wardrobe.*

He hit the PRINT command and Miranda reached for the list as it came out of the printer. "Okay," she said, "now all we have to do is go through your mom's list and compare it to this one."

"'Make Hillridge Beautiful,'" Gordo read from Mrs. McGuire's list. "'Join our volunteers picking up litter and planting flowers.'"

"I've seen some cute boys doing that," Miranda pointed out.

"Yeah, but it's basically trash collection," Lizzie said. "And you have to wear those Day-Glo orange vests. No way."

"Scratch that," Miranda agreed. "How about Habitat for Hillridge? You build houses for people who can't afford their own. They do great work, and lots of hot guys join, because they usually teach all these cool building skills."

Lizzie thought it over.

On the minus side, I might have to wear a hard hat. On the plus side, maybe I could build a shed to stash the little rodent in.

"I'll definitely apply for that one," she said.

Gordo glanced at the list again. "Walking dogs for the animal shelter?"

"That's not bad," Miranda said encouragingly. "When you walk dogs, you meet lots of other people. Plus, you're helping these poor animals who've been cooped up in cages."

Lizzie began ticking off pros and cons. "Meeting people, good. Being nice to dogs, also good." She wrinkled her nose. "Cleaning up after them, not so good."

"You're a hard girl to please," Gordo observed. He scanned the list again. "Hey," he said, sounding interested, "the Hillridge Community Center is looking for volunteers for their summer programs—the kids' day camp, the computer center, the gym—"

"Lizzie, that'd be perfect!" Miranda interrupted. "All sorts of seriously hot guys work at the HCC in the summer."

"Mmm," Lizzie said dreamily.

One application to the HCC coming right up!

Lizzie picked one more job to apply for. Then her friends left and she sat down at the computer and began to fill out applications. This definitely wasn't going to be the relaxing summer she'd been looking forward to, she told herself. But maybe it wouldn't be so bad.

CHAPTER TWO

Two weeks later, Lizzie stood in her room getting ready for her first day of volunteer work. Since the Hillridge Community Center was the only place that had offered Lizzie a job, that was where she was going to work, three days a week. Common Grounds, the non-profit café, already had all the volunteers they could use. And Habitat for Hillridge had sent an e-mail saying they had a slot if her "skill set included a certificate in electrical wiring."

Doesn't shopping qualify
as a skill set?
How about accessorizing?

Now she glanced at her reflection in the mirror. She had on white Capri pants, clear jelly flip-flops, and a pink sleeveless top with a pink sparkly headband. Definitely a good look. HCC, here I come, she thought.

Half an hour later, Lizzie followed the WEL-COME, SUMMER VOLUNTEERS! signs into one of the HCC's meeting rooms. About twenty teens were milling around. Lizzie didn't recognize anyone. She suddenly missed Miranda and Gordo, big-time.

A woman with short, black hair introduced herself as Joy, the head of volunteers, then pointed to a white board where she'd written the places they could be assigned. Lizzie scanned the first column: gym, K-3 day camp, hiking club, computer center. That all sounded promising.

"We've tried to match your assignments to the interests you listed on your applications," Joy explained. "In some cases, however, we've just assigned people to the places where we have the greatest need."

Lizzie tried to remember the interests she'd mentioned. But she'd filled out three applications in a row, and now she wasn't sure what she had said on any of them.

A seriously cute boy was peering in through the open doorway.

"Uh, is this the meeting for summer volunteers?" Ethan Craft asked.

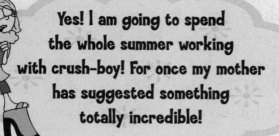

Yes! I am going to spend the whole summer working with crush-boy! For once my mother has suggested something totally incredible!

"It is. Come right in," Joy told him.

Lizzie thought she might pass out with happiness as Ethan sat down in the empty chair right next to her. "Yo, dude," he said.

"Hi, Ethan," she replied.

"Okay, let's get to your assignments," Joy said. "Marc Aranoff, the pool," she began.

"Yes!" Marc raised his fist, as if he'd just won a race.

"Ethan Craft," Joy said, "the gym."

"All right!" Ethan was clearly pleased with his assignment.

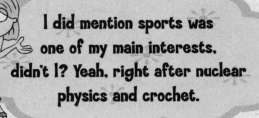

I did mention sports was one of my main interests, didn't I? Yeah, right after nuclear physics and crochet.

Lizzie immediately started praying to the fairy godmother of summer jobs.

Please, please, please let me be assigned to the gym!

Lizzie became more and more anxious as she waited for her name to be called. No one else had been assigned to the gym yet.

Lizzie held her breath as Joy reached the

Ms. "Donna Macey," Joy said, "the gym."

Lizzie shot a quick glance at Donna, and her heart sank.

Donna Macey was petite and slender, with long waves of shiny, brown hair and big, blue eyes. Ethan noticed, too. He called out, "Yo, Donna!" and gave her two thumbs-up.

"Lizzie McGuire, senior center," Joy said.

Please tell me this is not happening. Instead of working with Ethan, I'm going to be working with old people?

"Senior center?" Lizzie asked in disbelief. "Excuse me, but did you say *senior center?*"

Joy looked up over her clipboard. "Yes, Lizzie," she said. "You and Jasmine DeLong will be working in the senior center."

"But I didn't say anything about being interested in seniors," Lizzie protested. "I'm sure of it. I—" She shut her mouth. Everyone was staring at her, and she knew that what she had just said sounded awful. She was a volunteer, after all. Wasn't the whole point to go where you were needed?

Joy gave her an understanding smile, then returned to her list. By the time she'd finished the assignments, the adults in charge of the various programs had come into the conference room. Ethan and Donna trooped off with a guy who looked like a bodybuilder. And an outdoorsy bearded guy rounded up the volunteers assigned to trails.

At least I'll be working close to crush-boy, Lizzie consoled herself. She might run into Ethan in the hallways or at the snack machines.

"Lizzie McGuire and Jasmine DeLong, meet Ada Barron," Joy said.

Lizzie turned to face a tall, slim woman with chin-length, gray hair. She wore silver sandals and a straight-line sleeveless dress in a pale silvery fabric. She looked cool, comfortable, and totally classy, Lizzie thought. Jasmine, whose hair was woven into dozens of tiny braids, wore an embroidered top and low-rise jeans with a cell phone attached to the waistband.

"Hillridge just completed building our new senior center," Ada explained.

She led Lizzie and Jasmine outside to a small building just behind the HCC. It had a very modern design with a curving front wall made of glass blocks and wood. Lizzie knew it was good that the seniors had a new space of their own, but now she wouldn't even be in the same building as Ethan.

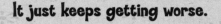
It just keeps getting worse.

"Here we are," Ada said, pushing open the door to the lounge. Lizzie felt her spirits lift at once. The lounge was a big, bright, cheerful room, with French doors that opened onto a garden. Outside, Lizzie could see shade trees, a terrace with chairs and rows of flowers, and, beyond them, the sparkling waters of a pool.

"The senior center has its own garden and pool and meeting rooms," Ada was saying. "We even have our own café and gym. But we share the auditorium, the computer center, and the darkroom in the main building."

Lizzie glanced around. There were probably about twenty seniors altogether, most sitting in groups of two or three.

"May I have your attention, everyone," Ada called. "I'd like to introduce you to our two new volunteers, Jasmine DeLong and Lizzie McGuire."

Lizzie and Jasmine both waved. Lizzie tried to smile, but Jasmine just looked bored.

"We set up activities based on the seniors' interests," Ada explained. "We'll have a choral group and a drumming group, plus water-aerobics, computer, painting, and swing-dancing classes. We have instructors for these activities, so we'd like you girls to assist them."

"I could use some assistance with this form," said a man in a colorful Hawaiian shirt. "The print is so small, I can barely read it."

"You don't have reading glasses?" asked the woman sitting next to him. She had honey-colored hair and wore a lacy white tunic over sky blue pants.

"I don't like reading glasses," the man said.

"You mean you're too vain to wear them," the woman translated.

"I'll help you," Lizzie intervened quickly. "What part do you want me to read?"

"Don't encourage him," the woman said. She took a pair of reading glasses from her purse and thrust them at the man. "Here, use these. It's better than asking someone else to do it for you. You should have filled out that form two weeks ago when everyone else did."

Muttering something about busybodies, the man took the glasses and began to fill out the form.

"Are you two married?" Lizzie asked the woman, curiously.

"Perish the thought! I never saw him before today," the woman said. "I'm Clarice, dear, and I believe his name is Dorcas."

"It's Marcus," the man retorted and glowered at Clarice.

"Lizzie," Ada said from the front of the room, "let me introduce you to Sandra Wolcott, our dance instructor."

Sandra, who had short, wavy brown hair and a round, curvy build, also had the straightest posture Lizzie had ever seen. She seemed to be about the same age as Lizzie's mom. She smiled and said, "I was hoping I'd get an assistant this summer. Do you think you can handle the music?"

As long as I don't have to dance!

"I'll try," Lizzie said.

Ten minutes later, Lizzie, Sandra, and the eight seniors who had signed up for the swing class were in the senior center's studio, a rectangular room with polished wood floors and mirrors lining one wall.

On Sandra's instructions, Lizzie plugged in a laptop with a CD drive and connected it to the speakers in the room. Sandra pulled up a screen that listed songs. "I'll call out a song, and then I'll need you to click on it," she explained. "For example, start with number three now."

Lizzie clicked on the third song title, and big-band swing music filled the room.

"Let's start with some warm-up exercises," Sandra said.

Lizzie watched as the seniors stretched. Clarice and Marcus were both part of the group, as were a married couple named Grace and Harry.

"Hips front and side and back and side," Sandra chanted. "Now switch. Everyone, shake your booty!"

All the seniors except Marcus energetically shook their backsides.

"Shake it!" Clarice snapped. Marcus gave a reluctant little wiggle. Lizzie tried not to smile.

Sandra asked Lizzie to pause the music. "We're going to be doing Lindy Hop swing," Sandra explained, "since that's what most of you have experience in, though we won't get into any aerial moves."

Then Sandra taught a pattern in which the couple moved toward each other, joined hands, swiveled, and then the man spun the woman. It didn't look like much when they were walking through the steps. But with music, suddenly everyone was dancing and looking as if they were having a great time. Lizzie thought it was totally cool.

The hour flew by. After class, Lizzie went outside for a break and saw a woman named Harriet walking swiftly, elbows swinging and hips swaying. She looks like a duck walking really fast, Lizzie thought.

"It's power walking. Walk your way into strength and stamina! Try it!" Harriet barked in such an authoritative voice that Lizzie began to power walk.

"Chin up, elbows bent, chin *up*!" Harriet ordered.

Lizzie lifted her chin higher and promptly walked into a hedge.

"Whoa!" said a familiar voice as Lizzie crashed through the greenery. Ethan Craft and Donna Macey were sitting on the other side of the hedge, eating sandwiches. "You must be really hungry, dude," Ethan said.

Was it walk your way into *strength and stamina* or *maximum humiliation?*

CHAPTER THREE

Gordo was the last intern to show up at the *Chronicle* offices on Monday morning. He followed the receptionist's directions to the office of Jerome Parrish, deputy editor.

Gordo stepped inside. Sitting on the edge of the desk was a man in his thirties, his tie loosened at the throat, the sleeves of his white shirt rolled up.

"David Gordon?" the man asked. "I'm Jerome. I'll be running the Youth Page and you'll be reporting to me. I believe you already know the other two interns from your school?"

Sitting next to Jerome and flashing a megawatt-phony smile was Kate Sanders, aka the Queen of Mean. Gordo couldn't think of anyone he disliked more. Was he really going to have to spend the next month working with the she-beast? The other Hillridge Junior High intern was Larry "Tudge" Tudgeman, who easily took the prize for the school's biggest geek.

"Let me introduce you to the two interns from Jefferson Junior High," Jerome said. "Lorene Hopkins will write movie reviews, and Ingrid Samson will be our photographer. Kate will be writing a fashion column, and Larry, a computer-gaming column. And you, Mr. Gordon, will write a weekly column on summer jobs for teens."

"Uh, that's not what I proposed on my

application," Gordo said. "I wanted to write a column on ways to avoid the social cliques in junior high."

Jerome glanced down at his notes. "That's true. We, meaning the *Chronicle* staff, didn't think that would work for the Youth Page. So, instead, you'll be interviewing other junior high kids. Find an interesting angle on what they're doing for the summer. Got it?"

"Got it," Gordo said. It didn't sound like he had much choice.

"Good. Next item: procedure. Every week each one of you is responsible for turning in an article. Ingrid, you'll accompany the reporters to photograph their stories."

Ingrid nodded. She was definitely interesting, Gordo decided. She had a thick mane of sand-colored hair that looked as if she hadn't bothered to brush it. And while the rest of them were dressed neatly, Ingrid wore an open denim shirt over a worn green T-shirt and jeans. She didn't look like she could be bothered to impress anyone. Kate was wearing a little black dress and pearl earrings, and her blond hair was up in some sort of sophisticated twist. Lorene wore a short, flowered summer dress. Her brown, shoulder-length hair hung loose to her shoulders. She smiled at Gordo, and he smiled back.

"But," Jerome continued, "no one turns in work and assumes that we print it. You turn it in, we critique it, and then you revise it. Is that clear?"

They all nodded. He smiled at them. "Good, then let me show you your office."

Gordo wasn't sure what he expected, but it sure wasn't a dingy closet with a desk and a filing cabinet. A single rolling chair sat at the desk, which held a computer and a phone.

"I know it's not exactly glamorous," Jerome

told them. "It was a storage room until yesterday. Fact is, we don't have any spare offices. So you each get your own drawer in the filing cabinet. Other than that, you share everything in here. You'll probably write your articles at home, but you should save them to this computer so they can be edited. Understood?"

The five interns nodded.

"Then I suggest you get busy on your first article," Jerome told them. "Be ready to present drafts on Wednesday morning at nine. E-mail me if you run into problems."

"Wow," Lorene said softly when Jerome had left the room. "I didn't realize we'd be on our own so much."

"That's how it is for real reporters," Kate said. As if she actually knew anything about it. "Ingrid, I need to do a photo shoot of summer fashions. I want you at Kirkland Park tomorrow morning at ten."

Ingrid looked at Kate as if she were an interesting insect. "That's nice," she said.

Kate's eyes narrowed. "Your job is to be our photographer. I'm giving you your first assignment. What's the problem?"

"The problem is that I'm your photographer, not your servant. I like to be asked," Ingrid told her.

Tudge's eyes went wide with amazement, and Gordo almost whooped with delight. Before Kate could get another word in, he said, "Ingrid, could you give me some time tomorrow afternoon? I'm not sure who my first interview will be, but I can let you know in the morning."

"Sounds good," Ingrid said. She scrawled a phone number and handed it to Gordo. "That's my cell. Call me. What about you, Lorene?"

"I'm cool," Lorene said. "I'm going to catch that new teens-find-monsters-in-their-lockers flick tonight. I'll get some promotional shots from the movie theater."

"Larry?" Ingrid asked.

"I'm going to report on a new game—*Prey of Mantis*. I can scan in the cover of the box. No photo needed."

"Okay." Ingrid looped her camera bag onto her shoulder. "I'm out of here."

"What about my fashion shoot?" Kate demanded.

Ingrid wrote down something for her. "That's my e-mail address. Write me when you can figure out how to ask politely."

Gordo couldn't control himself. "Oooo! Someone just got burned," he crowed.

"Shut up, Gor-dork!" Kate snapped.

Tudge turned to her with an earnest expression. "Photographers can be very temperamental, Kate," he explained. "Artistic egos and all that."

Kate let out a howl of frustration. Gordo and Lorene left her sitting at the desk, with Tudge trying to comfort her.

"Is she always that entertaining?" Lorene asked Gordo.

He grinned. "You haven't seen anything yet. Kate is totally used to getting her way."

"Well, maybe this is the summer when that changes," Lorene replied.

"That," Gordo assured her, "would be a miracle."

Lorene's smile got wider. "I'm not sure I'll ever like Kate, but I think you and I are going to get on just fine. *Ciao*."

She left then, leaving Gordo to wonder what that "get on just fine" really meant.

That afternoon, Lizzie met Gordo outside Alejandra's restaurant.

"How goes it?" Gordo asked. "Did you

survive the first day of summer jobness?"

"It was okay," Lizzie replied, "but it wasn't what I expected."

"Neither was mine," Gordo said.

"Miranda sure lucked out," Lizzie said, feeling a surge of envy. "I can't believe her aunt's restaurant is right across the street from Kirkland Park."

"So?" Gordo asked.

"So Kirkland was just renovated. It has a skate park, a new amphitheater, and an outdoor movie screen," Lizzie explained. "It's practically the only cool place to hang out in Hillridge. And you know what that means."

Gordo looked confused. "No. What does it mean?"

How can a complete brainiac be so incredibly clueless?

"Miranda is working in Hottie Central," Lizzie explained.

Gordo just shook his head and opened the door to the restaurant.

They saw Miranda at once. She was wearing a white apron and a bandanna and carrying a plastic tub that was filled with dirty dishes.

"Welcome to Alejandra's," Miranda said, "where the food is great, but the dishwashing staff is seriously lacking."

"You need help with that?" Gordo asked, stepping toward her.

"No, I got it," said Miranda. "Have a seat. I'll be back in a minute."

Lizzie and Gordo sat down, and a dark-haired waiter took their orders for smoothies. As he started to make the fruit drinks, two guys got up, grabbed their boards, and headed out to the park.

"I told you," Lizzie whispered to Gordo. "Hottie Central!"

"Will you forget that for a minute?" Gordo asked. "Look at this place. It's amazing."

It was, Lizzie realized. The front room of the restaurant, the taco and smoothie bar, was nice enough. It had a gleaming wood bar, cool hexagonal tables, and great posters on the walls. It opened into a courtyard paved in brick, with lush green plants everywhere. And on the other side of the courtyard, Lizzie could see the real Alejandra's—what looked like an ultrahip restaurant.

"Wow," Lizzie said.

Miranda reappeared then, looking mussed and tired. "I thought I was going to be a hostess, taking reservations, seating people at elegant tables. You know what I've done all day? Bussed tables and filled in for the dishwasher that my aunt still hasn't hired."

"Patience, *chica*," said the waiter behind the counter as he handed Lizzie and Gordo their smoothies.

"This is my cousin, Hector," Miranda explained. "He's in college, so he gets to be a waiter and get tips."

"Hey, I paid my dues," Hector said. "I started working in my mom's last restaurant when I was twelve, and all I did was bus dishes for two years."

"This restaurant is so gorgeous," Lizzie said. "And you're right across the street from Kirkland. Miranda, you are in the heart of Hottie Central!"

Miranda rolled her eyes. "Trust me, skate-boarding hotties don't get too excited about a girl carrying dirty dishes around. How are your jobs?"

Gordo told them about his first day at the paper and how Ingrid had dissed Kate.

"I like this Ingrid already," Lizzie said.

Gordo looked at Miranda hopefully. "I've got to write about summer jobs. Can I start with a column on yours?"

"No way," Miranda said. "At least not until my job improves."

"What about you, Lizzie?" Gordo asked.

Lizzie told them about her first day at the community center. "There's nothing wrong with the seniors," she explained. "It's just that it's not what I was hoping for."

"Understood," Miranda said at once. "Major disappointment."

"Can you get a transfer?" Gordo asked.

"Maybe," Lizzie said. "But then I'd feel really bad. Jasmine already made it clear she doesn't like it. I don't want the seniors to think I don't like them either. I *do* like them."

"So you're going to stick this assignment out?" Miranda asked.

"I guess so," Lizzie answered unhappily. "I don't think I have a choice."

"Look on the bright side," Gordo said. "At least you guys aren't working with Kate."

Lizzie and Miranda grinned at each other. "True," they agreed.

"And there's one thing we can all look forward to," Miranda added. "The annual summer solstice block party is Wednesday night. Even if our jobs are a grind, at least we can party this week."

Lizzie frowned. "I wonder if I can pay Matt *not* to go to that."

"That's right," Gordo said, laughing. "At last summer's party, he somehow got you totally coated in blueberry salsa."

Lizzie rolled her eyes and glanced at the neon clock on the wall. "I'd better go. I promised my mom I'd be home in time for dinner."

"I'll walk you," Gordo offered.

He and Lizzie left the restaurant. They were about to turn toward Lizzie's house, when she said, "Let's stop in the skate park for a few minutes, okay?"

They made their way to the rim of the park. It looked like a giant cement bowl with ramps and grooves cut into its steep sides. Skateboarders were zipping by in every direction and at amazing speeds.

Lizzie and Gordo stood watching. "They're awesome," Gordo marveled. "I'm okay on a level surface, but I'd face-plant if I ever tried to go down some of those walls."

Lizzie's eyes widened. She couldn't believe all the insanely cute guys.

This is heaven! Major hottie sightings— in every direction!

Her heart nearly skipped a beat as a skateboarder zoomed past and flashed her a dazzling white smile.

"Gordo," Lizzie said, stunned, "that way-cool guy who just went by—he smiled at me."

Gordo did not seem to think this was earth-shattering news. He shrugged as they turned to leave.

"Well, maybe you'll see him again."

Please let me see him again, please!

CHAPTER FOUR

On Wednesday, Lizzie's morning at the senior center went by quickly. She helped out with a painting class, a stretch class, and water aerobics.

Between classes she hung out in the lounge, getting to know the seniors. They were an interesting group. Marcus had been a journalist before he retired. Grace and her husband, Harry, owned a shop that sold gourmet foods. William still worked part-time as a voice coach for actors. Harriet, the wiry power walker, turned out to be an ex-cop.

There was one senior, though, whom Lizzie couldn't get a handle on. She seemed younger than the others, and always sat off by herself. Something about her seemed sad.

"Do you think she's all right?" Lizzie asked Jasmine.

Jasmine glanced at the woman. "Her name is Rosa. She swam a couple of laps this morning. She seemed fine."

"Does she speak English?" Lizzie asked.

Jasmine shrugged. "She seemed to understand when the lifeguards announced free swim." Jasmine's cell phone rang, and she answered. "Zeke!" she said, her face brightening. "You drove a Hummer? How immense was it?

"Zeke's my boyfriend," she explained to Lizzie after she hung up. "He's sixteen and he's got the absolute best summer job."

"What is it?" Lizzie asked.

"He's parking cars at Rivenoak. Zeke's totally into autos."

Rivenoak, Lizzie knew, was the ritziest country club in Hillridge. Still, spending your whole summer parking cars?

"I wanted to work there, too," Jasmine said wistfully. "But I'm only fifteen, and all their help has to be at least sixteen."

That explained why Jasmine wasn't into her job. Lizzie was going to ask if Jasmine had considered transferring to another part of the HCC, when her cell phone rang again.

Jasmine flipped it open. "A Bentley?" she asked. "You have got to be kidding! What color is it?"

Am I missing something, or are cars really that thrilling?

Lizzie sighed and gave up on talking to Jasmine. She glanced at her watch. It was almost noon. And she was planning to have lunch in the café in the main building. Maybe she would see Ethan Craft.

Lizzie all but ran to the café. Ethan was not only there, but he was by himself. He was wearing khaki shorts and a blue T-shirt that was the same shade as his eyes. A choker of blue, white, and green beads made his tanned skin look even more golden than usual.

Lizzie sent up a quick, silent plea to the fairy godmother of summer: for once, let me and Ethan totally click.

Lizzie walked up to her crush-boy and said supercasually, "Hey, Ethan."

Ethan glanced up at her. "Yo, dude."

Then there an awkward silence, as Lizzie tried to think of something to say.

Lizzie noticed that Ethan was holding something—a typed sheet of paper. "What are you reading?" she asked.

"It's slammin'—a sneak preview of the Youth Page fashion column. Kate wrote it," Ethan said. "It's going to be in Friday's paper. And look at these photos!"

He flipped the page. Every photo was of Kate in a different outfit. "Are these pics awesome, or what?"

"I guess," Lizzie said, unenthusiastically.

Ethan looked up at her, an earnest expression on his tanned face. "Which one do you think is the best?" he asked. "Kate in this totally babelicious dress or the one where she's in shorts and her legs are, like, so long?"

ARGH! The she-beast strikes again!

"Um, Ethan, I've got to buy lunch and get back to the senior center," Lizzie managed to say. "Later, okay?"

"Whatever." Ethan didn't even look up. He was totally absorbed in the Kate photos.

Lizzie stood on line and ordered a peanut butter and jelly sandwich.

The fairy godmother of summer obviously has a warped sense of humor.

* * *

"Watch out, bubble brain!" Matt exclaimed as he made his way toward Lizzie at the summer solstice block party that night.

Lizzie stepped aside. Her brother was carrying a paper plate piled high with gooey cheese nachos.

"You didn't have to take so much," she said.

"I'm a growing boy," the rodent said in his most innocent tone.

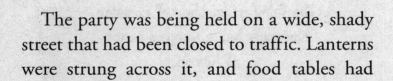

That's actually a scary thought. If he grows, there'll be more of him!

The party was being held on a wide, shady street that had been closed to traffic. Lanterns were strung across it, and food tables had been set up near barbecues, where most of the adults congregated. Folding chairs were scattered around, and a band, made up of a group of parents, was playing on a small stage.

Miranda walked up to Lizzie with two drinks in her hand. "Cherry soda for you and ginseng cream for me."

"Thanks," Lizzie said, but she was still glaring at Matt. "Why did my twerpy little brother have to show up at this party?"

"He lives here?" Miranda guessed.

"The band doesn't sound half-bad," Gordo said, coming up to Lizzie and Miranda with a slice of watermelon. He nodded at the stage. "They can actually play."

"We should go dance," Miranda said, already starting to move toward the stage.

"I'm going to finish my watermelon." Gordo headed for one of the chairs.

Lizzie, thinking of Sandra's swing classes,

tried to do a triple step. She concentrated on her feet, but couldn't make the triple-step rhythm work to the beat coming from the stage.

She glanced up, looking for Miranda but instead found herself staring at the boy who'd smiled at her in the skate park.

"Hi," she said. She'd recognize that smile anywhere. Now that he didn't have his helmet on, she saw that he had straight brown hair, buzzed on top but a little long in the back, a skateboarder cut. A spray of freckles dusted the bridge of his nose and cheeks. He seemed much more clean-cut now, wearing a short-sleeved rugby shirt and jeans. He was, Lizzie decided, totally adorable.

"Hi." He held out a hand to her. "I'm Josh Russell."

"Lizzie McGuire," she replied as she shook his hand. "Did you just move to the neigh-borhood?"

**Please say yes.
Please!**

"Just for the summer," he told her. "I'm staying with my grandmother." He nodded to a short, gray-haired woman, who was helping herself to some salad. A leash, looped around her wrist, was attached to a tiny poodle.

"That's your grandmother?" Lizzie said. "I think she lives on the other end of my street. I'm sure I've seen her walking her dog."

"Yeah, that's Precious," Josh explained, "the love of her life."

"There you are!" Miranda emerged from the crowd. She glanced at Josh, then shot Lizzie a meaningful look. "I was wondering why you weren't dancing."

Lizzie found herself blushing. "Miranda,

this is Josh Russell. He's staying with his grandmother for the summer."

"Cool," Miranda said. She smiled at Josh. "So where do you really live?"

"San Francisco," Josh told them. "I figured that if I hung out here for a couple of months, I could escape the fog. You can't imagine how cold and dreary it makes things. Totally wrecks your summer."

Lizzie couldn't stop smiling. Josh seemed so nice and interesting.

Not to mention undeniably hot!

"Gordo and I saw Josh at the skate park," Lizzie explained to Miranda. She turned to Josh. "Miranda's aunt owns a restaurant right across from Kirkland."

"Yeah, it's called Alejandra's," Miranda said. "You should stop in. We serve killer tacos."

"You work there?" Josh asked, sounding interested.

Miranda nodded. "My summer job. I thought restaurant work was going to be glamorous and sophisticated. Instead, I've been filling in for the dishwasher."

"Hey, don't knock dishwashers," Josh teased. "That was my job last summer in my dad's restaurant."

Miranda's eyes widened with interest. She gave Lizzie a familiar look—a look that Lizzie considered dangerous. It meant Miranda was concocting a plan.

"You know," Miranda said to Josh, "if you have any free time and you want to earn some money, my aunt is looking to hire a part-time dishwasher."

Josh laughed. "Then I really would feel like

I was back in the Bay Area. I don't know. I'll think about it."

"Sounds good," Miranda said. She gave Lizzie that look again.

"Hey, what happened to the band?" Miranda asked. "I just realized the music stopped."

Lizzie turned to the stage. It was empty, and the crowd was quiet.

Miranda glanced at her watch. "It's only nine. It's too early for the music to be over."

Lizzie's mom came over then to ask if she wanted a sweater.

"I'm fine, Mom," Lizzie said. "But thanks."

She realized that her mother was no longer looking at her, but gazing toward the stage with one of those goofy, sentimental "mom" expressions. "Oh, doesn't he look adorable," Mrs. McGuire murmured.

Lizzie had a very bad feeling. She turned

toward the stage and gasped. "Oh, no. He can't. Mom, you can't let him!"

Matt was on the stage, Lanny by his side. He was standing over a double turntable.

Matt grabbed the microphone. "Good evening, neighbors!" he began. "You have just listened to the excellent sounds of the parents' band. But I thought you might like to hear something a little more— contemporary."

Matt turned on both turntables and began spinning vinyl disks, scratching and, in Lizzie's opinion, making the most awful racket. Then he began to rap.

"Now my life's not bad, though not exactly rad,
My problem's simply this: my weirdo older sis.
She thinks the bathroom's for her stuff
And there's always much too much
Lip gloss, moisturizer, zit cream, deodorant—"

"Make him stop!" Lizzie shrieked. She was dimly aware of Lanny bopping along in time to Matt's humiliating rap, and the sound of laughter all around her.

"—*conditioner, detangler, eye shadow, and blush*
pore cleaners, nail polish, pastel powder puffs—"

"That's it!" Lizzie cried. She jumped up onto the stage and pulled the electrical cords out of the socket. Then, she turned to her brother. "You obnoxious, little pointy-headed weasel," she began, advancing on him.

"Now, Lizzie." Matt put his hands up in defense and began backing away.

What stopped Lizzie wasn't the panic in Matt's eyes. It was Josh, standing in front of the stage, staring at her in disbelief.

Want to make an unforgettable impression on a guy? Try losing it in front of the entire neighborhood.

"Lizzie, Matt." Suddenly, their mom was onstage, her voice quiet but firm. "Come on, both of you. I think it's time we went home."

Okay, before this, the humiliation was intense but not complete. Now it's complete.

Lizzie fled from the stage and ran toward her house, sure she would never be able to face Josh again.

CHAPTER FIVE

Lizzie didn't speak to her brother the next day, even when he said he was sorry.

On Friday morning when she went down to breakfast, Matt was looking disgustingly cheerful. "Good morning, everyone," he said, giving them all a toothy smile. "I have an announcement. Since our performance at the block party was so successful, Lanny and I are forming an entertainment company. We already have our first gig: Seth Seligman's birthday party."

"I thought Seth was only four," Mr. McGuire said.

"He'll be five on Sunday," Matt said. "The party is going to have two wading pools and an ocean theme. Lanny and I are already researching music about water and fish."

"As long as it's not about your sister," Mrs. McGuire warned. "That was not acceptable."

Got that, pea brain?

"I know." Matt looked serious. "I'd like you all to spread the word that McGuire Music and Entertainment—aka McGuire M & E— is now accepting bookings. Lizzie, do you think you could give out my cards at the community center?"

Lizzie gave him a toothy smile. "Not in this lifetime," she said, and left the table.

Gordo arrived at the *Chronicle* offices, made himself a cup of decaf, and went into the meeting room. Lorene was the only one there.

"Morning," she said. She was sipping a latte and making notes on a yellow legal pad.

"Hi," Gordo said. "How's it going?"

"Okay," she answered, her attention still on her notes. She wrote for a few moments, then looked up at him. "Gordo," she said slowly, "you're pretty easy to talk to."

"I am?" Gordo said. "Thanks."

"I was wondering if I could ask you a question," she said. "A personal question."

"Shoot," Gordo said, feeling slightly nervous, though he wasn't sure why.

"This is kind of a strange question," Lorene said. She sounded nervous, too. "There's this guy—let's call him Hypothetical Guy—and I haven't known him long. We're suddenly around each other a lot, and I think he's totally amazing. But he doesn't seem to notice me."

"Listen, Lorene," Gordo said. "I'm not the best person to ask. You might not believe this, but I haven't had all that much experience dating. I don't know what to tell your friend."

Lorene wasn't discouraged. "Well, just tell me this. Do you think I should do something forthright and honest, like go up to him and say, 'I'm completely crushing on you'?"

"No," Gordo said quickly, in spite of himself. "That will only work if he feels the same way. If he doesn't, it will scare him off and ruin any chance you might have of really getting to know him. You've got to be subtler."

"That makes complete sense," Lorene said, smiling at him. Gordo realized she had a very pretty smile. "Thanks."

Ingrid, Tudgeman, and Kate soon took their places at the table, and Jerome began the meeting. "Kate, you wrote a good column on summer fashions, and the photos illustrate it nicely."

"Oh, I totally agree," Tudge said, smiling at Kate, who ignored him.

"Larry," Jerome went on, "great article on the new game."

"All-righty!" Tudge said, looking pleased.

"Lorene, good movie review, but you give away too much of the plot."

"I'll fix it," Lorene said, making a note on her legal pad.

"David," Jerome finished, "I was bored with this description of the kid working in the burger joint."

Gordo felt his face flame with embarrassment. "Well, it's kind of a boring job," he admitted. "But that's what's out there. When you're in junior high, most of the available jobs are the dregs."

"That may be," Jerome said, "but I can't have you boring our readers. Either find an interesting way to write about it or find another topic." Jerome closed his notebook. "Get to it, people. I want your revised pieces in by the end of the day."

Gordo started for home to think about a new approach to his article.

"I have an announcement," Ada said, moments after Lizzie arrived at the senior center. "It's clear to me that we've got a tremendously talented group. So I've arranged for us to have Talent Night in three weeks. We'll be practicing and performing in the auditorium in the main building."

This was greeted with great enthusiasm by all the seniors. All except Rosa. She sat by herself in the far corner of the room and seemed to have no reaction at all to the announcement.

Lizzie went over to talk with her. "Hi, Rosa," she said. "How are you?"

Rosa shrugged.

"Talent Night sounds like fun," Lizzie went on. "Do you have a talent—something you'd like to do for the show?"

"Oh, no." Rosa spoke very softly.

"You don't sing or dance?" she asked.

Rosa shook her head.

Lizzie grinned. "How about drumming? I can imagine you really banging on a drum."

Rosa laughed. "No drums."

"Then I hope you'll come watch. We'll need someone in the audience."

Something on the other side of the room caught Rosa's eye. She got to her feet and crossed the room to a bookshelf where a large black-and-white cat lay sprawled. Rosa began to pet it, and the cat rubbed its head against Rosa's hand, clearly loving the attention. Lizzie had never noticed the cat before. Had it been there all along?

Hmm . . . maybe I have to work on my powers of observation.

"Lizzie and Jasmine," Ada said, summoning them, "I need you to find out what kind of scenery and props each act will need. Then go to the auditorium and talk to Colin."

"Who's Colin?" Jasmine asked.

"Colin Lang is our one and only stage-hand," Ada explained. "He's in charge of lighting and sound, and he builds sets. So don't let any of the performers ask for anything too complicated."

Lizzie and Jasmine took notes on what the performers wanted. Then they walked over to the main building.

The auditorium was dark. At first, Lizzie thought it was empty, but then she saw light beneath one of the thick stage curtains.

She walked down to the stage. "Hello," she called out. "Um, Colin? Is anyone there?"

She heard movement behind the curtain. Then the curtain parted, the lights in the auditorium went on, and Lizzie was staring at Colin Lang.

Lizzie figured he was probably her age, but he didn't look quite like anyone she knew. Tall and slender, he wore glasses with thin blue metal rims. He had dark hair that was slicked back, and he wore a long-sleeved shirt open at the neck over worn, flared jeans. It was a different look, not jock or skateboard cool, but not nerdy either.

Let's just say he's intriguing and a little mysterious.

"What's up?" Colin asked, sitting on the edge of the stage.

"We have lists of what all the acts will need for Talent Night," Lizzie said.

Jasmine's cell phone rang. "Here." She thrust her list at Lizzie. "Zeke? You're in a Maserati? What model is it? You're kidding— the 3200 GT?"

Lizzie gave Colin an apologetic shrug. "She's going to be on for a while."

Colin took the pages from her and looked

them over. "The drumming group needs chairs and a rising moon?" he asked.

"They want to drum up the moon," Lizzie explained. "So can you do some sort of big full moon that rises behind them and lights up the stage as they drum?"

"Maybe," Colin said as he continued to look over the list. "The swing dancers don't need anything except their music and lighting. That's good. The choral group wants risers to stand on. I may be able to borrow those from the gym. Harriet wants a slide of a track projected behind her?"

Lizzie nodded. "She's going to give a talk and a demo of power walking."

"Right." Colin glanced at the last item on the list. "And who is William and why does he need 'a picket fence with tree, tree swing that works, and impending rainstorm'?"

"William's an actor and voice coach," Lizzie

explained. "He's going to read a piece about life in the country that ends with rain sweeping in. So I think he needs some lightning and distant thunder."

"Let me see what I can come up with." Colin glanced at the list again. "So it's really only two acts that need props, plus Harriet's slide. Tell Ada I can probably get all this done, but I'll need an assistant to help with all the sound and lighting cues."

"I can help you," Lizzie said before she had a chance to think about it.

She wasn't quite sure why she had volunteered so quickly.

Is it just that helping Colin means hanging out with someone under the age of sixty?

"So what kind of help do you need?" Lizzie asked.

"Do you know how to run a lighting or sound board?" Colin asked.

"No," Lizzie admitted.

"Can you rig a sun to rise?"

"Nope." Lizzie was starting to get a little frustrated.

"Cut a tree from plywood?"

Lizzie shook her head.

Colin did not look pleased. "If I make the props, can I trust you to paint them?"

Only if I can trust you to stop acting like such a jerk!

"I think I can manage that," Lizzie said frostily. Colin might be intriguing, but he wasn't exactly nice.

"Fine." Colin sounded resigned. "Tell Ada I can use your help if she can spare you."

"Fine," Lizzie said, but what she wanted to say was, "Tell her yourself."

She was definitely having second thoughts. Colin hadn't smiled once during their conversation. He had just been stiff and businesslike. And now he was acting all bossy and superior.

Maybe he's not nearly as intriguing as I thought. And why do I even care? This is the summer of Josh Russell, skateboarding hottie!

* * *

"So I finally escaped a seniors-only summer," Lizzie told Miranda that afternoon, as they sat at the taco bar. "Only I think I may have just volunteered to work with someone who's not even as interesting as the seniors. He's kind of cute, but he seems like a jerk."

Miranda's expression was only half sympathetic. Her dark hair was sticking out at odd angles from her headband, and the apron she wore was smudged and stained. "At least you didn't break a forty-dollar bottle of truffle oil," Miranda said.

"Forty dollars?" Lizzie asked.

"Yup. It took me over an hour to clean up. And my aunt was really mad because she'd special-ordered it from France for a dish she was going to make tonight." Miranda sighed heavily. "I'm really beginning to wonder why I'm working here."

Hottie Central, remember? Some people just don't appreciate a good location.

"Okay, that's the perfect starting point for your interview," Gordo said as he walked toward them.

"Gordo," Miranda said in a dangerous tone, "if you interview me today, my aunt will never speak to me again, and I will personally dismantle your computer."

"Okay, okay," Gordo agreed. He could tell when Miranda was serious. "Lizzie?" he asked hopefully.

"Sorry, Gordo," Lizzie said as Hector set down the taco she'd ordered. "You're going to have to find someone else for your column."

"Right," Gordo said. He looked a little depressed. Lizzie was about to apologize, when Gordo saw someone sitting at the far end of the taco bar. "Later," he said.

Lizzie and Miranda watched as he sat down next to a girl with medium-length brown hair.

"Who's that?" Miranda whispered to Lizzie.

"Search me," Lizzie whispered back. "But obviously Gordo knows her. He ditched us for her." Lizzie felt a pang of something.

It must be heartburn.

Just then, the door to the restaurant opened and Josh came in. "Hey, Miranda." He nodded at Lizzie. "What's up?"

Lizzie could only nod back; she'd just bitten into her taco. He'd spoken to her! Hopefully he'd forgotten about the incident at the block party.

"Hey, is your aunt still looking for a part-time dishwasher?" Josh asked Miranda.

"Yeah," she answered, with a smile at Lizzie. "Come on, I'll introduce you."

Miranda dropped Josh in the kitchen and hurried back to the table.

"Oh. My. Gosh." Lizzie said. "One of Hillridge's ultimate hotties might work here!"

"Well, he's definitely cute," Miranda said. Lizzie looked at her.

Miranda blushed and cleared her throat. "Do you like him?" she asked.

"Of course. Have you seen him? Plus, he seems nice." Lizzie said. "Besides, Ethan's unlikely. He told me how 'babelicious' Kate's photos were."

"Eeew." Miranda made a face. "Really?"

Lizzie nodded glumly.

"Don't worry," Miranda said. "I'll make sure Josh notices you. By the time this summer's over, you'll forget all about Ethan Craft."

Yeah, and cats will play water polo. Then again, who knows? There could be some very wet cats in this town.

CHAPTER SIX

On Saturday afternoon, Matt and Lanny set up a card table between the two wading pools in Seth Seligman's backyard. About a dozen four-year-olds in bathing suits were racing around the yard.

Matt took the portable CD player from his backpack and put it on the table. It was not the easiest task. Like Lanny, Matt was wearing rubber flippers on his hands. Both boys were dressed in big cardboard fish costumes that they had made the night before.

Next, Matt put in the CD he had burned that morning. It was filled with songs about oceans, boats, and fish. "Happy birthday, Seth, and hello, everyone else!" Matt called.

"Look, dear," said one of the mothers to her son. "That nice fish is talking."

Matt wished he had a microphone. Since he didn't, he just kept talking loudly. "We're going to play some music for you," he explained. "And we're going to do some special fish dances."

The little kids paid no attention. They were too busy splashing.

"Ready, Lanny?" Matt asked.

Lanny nodded, and Matt pushed the CD player's ON button. A cheerful song about an octopus in a garden came on, and both Matt and Lanny started to dance. A little boy carried a bucket of water over to Matt and threw it at him. "So you can stay wet and keep breathing," he said.

Matt stopped dancing, ready to yell at the kid. But then he decided it was kind of a compliment. The kid must have thought he was a real fish.

The next song, "Row, Row, Row Your Boat," came on and Matt forgot about being soaked. He and Lanny had to pretend they were rowing.

Matt and Lanny rowed and sang, and a funny thing happened. The kids at the party started to pay attention. By the time the next song—about going surfing—played, all the kids were singing along and mimicking Matt and Lanny as they pretended to surf. Matt could see Seth's mother, smiling and clapping along with the beat. This was a blast, Matt decided. He was born to run McGuire's M & E.

Lizzie got off the bus and walked toward her house. It was a bummer that she had wasted a Saturday afternoon at the dentist's office, but at least she didn't have any cavities.

She was about a block from her house, when she came to a sudden halt. She couldn't believe it. Josh Russell was standing a few yards ahead, holding on to a leash attached to his grandmother's dog.

Maybe my luck is finally about to change!

"Hi," Lizzie said. "That's Precious, right?"

Josh nodded. "Yeah, my grandmother's watching some TV movie and asked if I'd take Precious for her afternoon walk."

"Is it okay if I walk with you?" Lizzie asked. "My house is just down the street."

"Sure," Josh said. He sounded easy and relaxed. His tone made Lizzie relax, too.

"So what happened at Alejandra's?" she asked. "Did you get the job?"

Josh gave a low laugh. "It wasn't hard. I think if a chimp had walked in there with a little sign saying *it* washed dishes, Alejandra would have hired it on the spot. She was pretty desperate. So I'm going to work three days a week. That way I can earn some money and do something besides hanging out on my board at Kirkland and driving my grandmother crazy."

This is a first! For once, I actually have something to talk about with a boy!

"Do you really?" Lizzie asked. "Drive your grandmother crazy, I mean."

Josh shrugged. "I'm always telling her I think she should get out and do things. And she's perfectly happy to stay home and walk the dog three times a day. I'm beginning to think maybe I should just let her do what she wants. What are you up to?"

"Nothing thrilling," Lizzie said, and told him about her dental appointment. "But," she went on as an idea came to her, "Miranda, Gordo, and I are all going to meet tonight at the Digital Bean around seven. We'll probably have smoothies there, and then we're going to the free outdoor movie in Kirkland Park. Do you want to come with?"

"Sure," he said. "I'll just tell my grandmother. I'll meet you at the Digital Bean at seven."

"See you then," Lizzie agreed. She let

herself into her house and walked very sedately up the stairs to her room. She shut her bedroom door, took off her shoes, stepped up onto her bed, and began jumping up and down, as if it were a trampoline.

"I asked a boy out, and he said yes!" she shouted with glee. "Josh Russell said yes!"

That evening Lizzie found Gordo and Miranda in their favorite little nook in the Bean. Lizzie pulled up a comfy stuffed chair and settled in.

"Is he here yet?" she asked Miranda.

"Is who here?" Gordo wanted to know.

"Not yet," Miranda told Lizzie. "Josh Russell, the skateboarder," she explained to Gordo. "Lizzie invited him to meet us here and go to the movie."

"You did?" Gordo looked impressed. "You actually asked a guy out?"

"Well, with two other friends along, it wasn't exactly like I was asking him on a date," Lizzie admitted.

Gordo nodded. "Good strategy. Casual, no pressure, but gives you a chance to get to know each other. Plus, Miranda and I can watch you two and see if we approve."

Miranda elbowed him lightly. "Don't say things like that. You'll make her nervous." She lowered her voice. "Here he comes now."

Josh walked over to their nook, carrying pink lemonade, and sat down in the empty chair across from Lizzie. Maybe because of what Gordo said, Lizzie felt awkward. She was relieved when Miranda began to talk.

"Aunt Alejandra says you're going to start at the restaurant on Monday?"

"Yeah," Josh said, "it should keep me out of trouble."

"Did you know Lizzie works at the senior center?" Miranda asked. "It's a great program."

Since when is Miranda so enthusiastic about the senior center?

"Josh, you should tell your grandmother about it," Miranda went on. "She might really like it."

"She'd never go," Josh said. "My grandmother doesn't leave the house without her dog. Precious goes everywhere she does."

"That's no problem," Miranda said at once. "The senior center understands how important pets are to seniors. They know a pet can be an older person's most important companion. So they totally welcome them."

"They do?" Lizzie asked. She couldn't think of anyone who brought pets to the center.

"Absolutely," Miranda said, giving Lizzie a look that clearly meant, Work with me on this—I'm doing it for you.

"Right," Lizzie said quickly. "You know, the pets who do come to the program are so mellow, I barely notice them."

Okay, so maybe I'm exaggerating a little.

"And—" Lizzie tried to come up with something appealing. "We have beautiful gardens that your grandmother might like."

"Exactly," Miranda said. "It's a totally peaceful, serene, relaxing place. Everyone who goes there loves it!"

"Well, Precious *is* pretty calm," Josh said thoughtfully. "Maybe I'll mention it to Gram and see if I can get her to try it out."

As long as you come with her!

Gordo just shook his head and said, "We'd better get going if we don't want to miss the movie."

They all trooped over to Kirkland Park and made their way to the big, open field that faced a giant outdoor screen. There were plenty of folding chairs, but Miranda opened a big picnic blanket so they could all stretch out under the stars.

Darkness was falling and the summer night felt soft and full of promise. Lizzie was suddenly very happy that she was going to spend the next couple of hours here with Miranda and Gordo and Josh.

She was happy, that is, until they arranged themselves on the blanket. Josh plunked down between Miranda and Gordo.

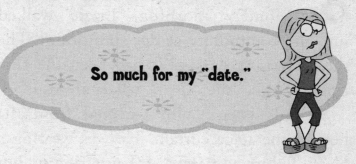

So much for my "date."

CHAPTER SEVEN

On Monday morning, Lizzie walked into the community center auditorium. The theater was as dark as it had been the first time. "Colin," she called, "where are you?"

Seconds later, Colin emerged from the behind the stage curtain. He was wearing a black T-shirt and jeans. He was skinny, but looked very strong.

For some reason, Lizzie imagined herself slow dancing with him.

"Are you working with me this morning?" he asked.

Lizzie snapped out of her daydream and nodded. "Ada set it up so that mornings, I help you out on the show. Afternoons, I'm back in the senior center."

Colin took this in, but didn't react. "What about Jasmine?" he asked.

"She is working on posters for the show and getting flyers into the local stores." Lizzie grinned. "I think Ada figured out that Jasmine has to do something where it doesn't matter if she keeps talking on her cell phone."

"There are paints back there." Colin motioned toward a corner of the backstage area. "Go to it."

It's nice to see you, too.

Soon, Lizzie was kneeling on a drop cloth on the stage, painting the picket fence that Colin had built for William's reading.

Lizzie found that it was fun to paint scenery. She liked watching the plywood form turn into a fence. She tensed a little as she heard Colin's footsteps behind her. Was he going to be grouchy again?

To her surprise, he knelt beside her. "That looks really good," he said. "Where did you learn to paint so well?"

"Grammar school?" Lizzie guessed.

"So art's your favorite subject?"

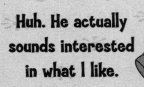

Huh. He actually sounds interested in what I like.

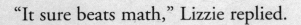

"It sure beats math," Lizzie replied.

"Definitely," Colin said with a laugh.

As Lizzie applied white paint to William's fence, Colin picked up a thin brush and dipped it in the gray paint. "If you just dab it on like this," he said, "you'll make the fence look weathered." He leaned across her to demonstrate, and his arm brushed hers.

Lizzie blushed. There was something really nice about the feel of his arm, warm and strong, touching hers. Colin turned and looked at her then, a curious expression in his dark eyes. But he didn't say anything. He just set the brush down and got up.

"The gray paint looks good," Lizzie said quickly. "I—I can't believe you already made this fence."

Colin shrugged and began to run a plane against the wood surface of William's tree. "Well, it's easier than making a real fence. All this stuff has to do is look convincing and not fall down. Careful, you're dripping paint," he told her, but he smiled at her when he said it.

Colin, Lizzie realized, was seriously handsome when he smiled. He had the nicest brown eyes.

Wow. He seems to get better and better looking.

The back door to the auditorium opened and Sandra came in, trailed by the swing class. "Can we use the stage to practice?" she asked. "I want my dancers to get used to the actual space where they'll perform."

Colin hesitated a moment and glanced at Lizzie. "We'll get back to this later?" he asked.

"Absolutely," Lizzie promised.

Colin gave her that smile again, and in that

instant Lizzie felt happier than she'd been all summer. If only Josh would smile at me like that, she thought.

Colin turned to Sandra and said, "Sure. Lizzie and I can move this stuff backstage."

It took some tugging and hauling on the drop cloths, but Lizzie and Colin got all their stuff out of the way. Sandra brought four couples onto the stage and began to mark out the dances with them.

"Lizzie, can you see to the music?" she asked. "And Colin, can you work the lights?"

Lizzie started the first song.

"Five, six, seven, eight," Sandra counted. "Rock-step, triple-step, triple-step, now push off, ladies, and slide."

The women were supposed to slide a few steps. Everyone did except Clarice, who scowled at Marcus and said, "You weren't holding me properly."

"You were pushing off on the wrong foot," Marcus told her.

"Let's try it again," Sandra said diplomatically. "You should all be moving in a straight line, toward the audience."

The rehearsal went on that way for the better part of an hour. By the time they were finished, everyone had the sequence down. They moved toward each other, swung and slid, and the men spun the women in a series of turns. Lizzie couldn't help but feel a little envious. She hadn't realized that partner dancing could be so cool. Then again, she'd never met anyone her age who danced swing or even knew what "Lindy Hop" meant.

I would be considered a total freak if people knew I wished I could move like a bunch of seniors.

Lizzie broke into wild applause as they finished their last dance.

"Weren't they terrific?" Lizzie asked Colin as the seniors filed out of the auditorium.

Colin shrugged and gave her a typical teenage-male response. "They're okay," he said. "If you like that kind of thing."

Lizzie was not having a good afternoon. Things started to slide downhill when she opened her purse in the lounge and found a little stack of business cards that read:

McGuire Music and Entertainment
for all occasions!
Call Matt McGuire: 555-6742

Lizzie tossed the cards on a table in disgust. She'd lost track of the number of times she'd told the little toad to keep his slimy hands out of her purse!

Is it too late to get my parents to ship El Twerpo off to summer camp?

She was distracted from these thoughts when she realized that the senior center had visitors: Josh, his grandmother, and Precious.

This is it—my big chance! Josh will see me working with the seniors, and he'll realize how wonderful I am!

Lizzie waved at Josh, but he didn't see her. "This is the lounge, Mrs. Russell," Ada was saying. "And we have our own pool, just beyond the garden. Would you like me to show you?"

"That'd be lovely," Josh's grandmother said, moving toward the doors that opened onto the center's garden. Precious trotted happily at her side.

Then everything happened so fast that Lizzie could barely follow it. Precious caught sight of the cat—the big, old fat cat that Lizzie had completely forgotten about. The dog barked at the cat, which had been sprawled out on top of a bookshelf. The cat arched up, hissing. Its tail fluffed, ears flat, and claws out, it leaped at poor little Precious's head.

A chase ensued, ending when the cat, backed up against a wall, suddenly spun around and raked the dog across the nose.

My big chance just went straight down the drain!

Precious whimpered in pain, and her mistress scooped her up.

Rosa picked up the furious cat and carried it outside.

"I'm so sorry, Mrs. Russell," Ada began.

"I've got to bring Precious to a vet," said Mrs. Russell.

Josh's green eyes were suddenly focused on Lizzie. He scowled. "I thought animals were welcome in here, that seniors brought their animal companions in all the time."

Lizzie felt awful. "Is that what Miranda said?" she asked in a small voice.

"Yeah, it is," he told her. "And you were right there and didn't say anything different."

Something tells me he's not getting the wonderful part.

"Lizzie, why—" Ada looked from Lizzie to Josh, and then seemed to think better of her question. "Never mind. Mrs. Russell, I'm so sorry this happened. By all means, have Precious checked out and have the vet bill me."

Josh's grandmother nodded stiffly, still holding the little dog in her arms. "We'd better go," she said as she and Josh left.

Lizzie decided there was nothing more she could do. She went outside, where she found Rosa petting the cat.

"So, you like cats," Lizzie said to Rosa.

"I like this cat," Rosa replied. "I think he knows what it's like to be lonely."

"Are you lonely?" Lizzie asked.

"Just this summer," Rosa said. "My sister Sofia and I have shared a house for years, but last month she went down to Mexico." Rosa smiled. "Her daughter is going to have a baby, and Sofia wants to be there for the birth. But I miss her."

"Do you two normally do a lot together?" Lizzie asked.

Rosa shrugged. "Some days." She shook her head. "My birthday is coming up, and every year Sofia would make me the most delicious *tres leches* cake. I know it's silly, but every time I think of my birthday without that cake, I want to cry."

Lizzie found herself touching Rosa's hand. "You must miss her a lot," she said. "But maybe you'll find some good things here this summer."

"I found a friend," Rosa said, stroking the cat. "That's a start."

But it wasn't enough, Lizzie thought as they brought the cat back inside.

That night, Lizzie called Miranda and told her about Rosa. "A *tres leches* cake is some sort of Mexican cake, right?"

"Mmm," Miranda said in a dreamy tone. "It's a creamy white cake soaked in three kinds of milk and topped with vanilla whipped cream. When they're made right, they're incredible."

"I know it would make Rosa really happy if I could get one for her birthday," Lizzie said. "Do you know anyone who makes them?"

"My aunt Alejandra might bake one. I'll ask her, but only if I get a piece of that cake."

"It's a deal," Lizzie replied.

Gordo felt a knot in his stomach as Jerome began the Tuesday morning editorial meeting. Last week, Jerome had told him his article was boring, and Gordo had spent hours rewriting it. Today, they'd discuss his second article. Gordo had his fingers crossed that this one was an improvement.

"Lorene," Jerome began. "Nice review of the sci-fi flick, but it would be stronger if you compared it to some other space movies."

Lorene nodded and jotted down a note on her pad. "Sounds good."

Jerome then praised Tudgeman's article. Tudge was so excited he started to do a little victory dance in his seat. He stopped abruptly as Kate said, "Please!" and shot him a withering look.

Jerome turned to Gordo next. "I like this article on the florist," Jerome began. "You managed to get an interesting angle."

"How could arranging flowers be interesting?" the she-beast asked.

"Actually, I interviewed your cousin Hal," Gordo said, knowing that Hal and Kate didn't get along. "This summer, Hal is working for Valerie's Flowers," Gordo explained to the others. "He researched something called the secret language of flowers on the Internet, and made up an ad. And now they're getting all these orders for symbolic bouquets."

"What are they?" Lorene asked, looking intrigued.

"Well, according to a kind of code that was popular in the Victorian times, every flower and most plants have a secret meaning. For example, Hal showed me a bouquet with ferns, which mean 'fascination,' lupine, which means 'imagination,' and yellow acacia, which means 'secret love.' Hal says it's the perfect gift from a secret admirer to someone they find fascinating or imaginative."

"Sounds juvenile to me," Kate said.

"I don't think so," said Lorene. "If I got a bouquet like that from a secret admirer, I'd be thinking about it for days."

"Me, too." Ingrid's admission surprised them all, mostly because Ingrid never said anything personal. "And look." She took photos of the different message bouquets out of a portfolio and set them on the conference table. "Hal made all of these while we were there, and each one is totally unique."

"Wow," Jerome said. "I might have to send one to my girlfriend. Nice shots, Ingrid. Excellent story, David."

Gordo smiled. He was finally getting the hang of this job.

Gordo spent the rest of the morning in the *Chronicle* offices, setting up interviews with other kids about their summer jobs and doing research in the archives.

By the time Gordo got back to the shared desk, the other interns were gone for the day. But someone had left something behind.

It was a bouquet, consisting of dark green ferns, purple lupine, and yellow acacia. Gordo remembered what Hal had called that particular arrangement: the perfect gift from a secret admirer.

Gordo picked up the bouquet, looking for some sort of note or address. There wasn't any. Had it been left here for him?

No, Gordo told himself. Not possible. Someone, though, had deliberately ordered a bouquet that was meant to be a message from a secret admirer. And Gordo couldn't help wondering who it was for.

CHAPTER EIGHT

"Matt, why are you and Lanny wearing sunglasses at the breakfast table?" Mrs. McGuire asked the next morning. "Is it too bright?" She peered up at the light fixture above the table.

Lizzie sighed. "The lights are fine, Mom," she said. "This has got to be connected to Matt's, uh, music business."

"Exactly," Matt said. "A music mogul never takes off his shades. They signal to the world just how cool we are."

Does anyone else have to put up with stuff like this at breakfast?

Mr. McGuire cast a doubtful look at his son. "Since you just tried to eat your cereal with a fork, maybe you should save the shades for outdoors."

The phone rang, and Matt, his shades still on, answered it. "Hello? Yes, you've reached McGuire Music and Entertainment. You want to book us for this weekend? Let me check with my agent. Lanny, are we available for a gig this Saturday?"

Lanny whipped an appointment book out of his pocket, checked it, then gave Matt a thumbs-up signal.

"I believe we can accommodate you," Matt said. He listened for a moment, then added, "Actually, that's less than we're usually paid, but I always leave the negotiations to my agent. Hold on."

Matt held the phone out to Lanny, who took it from him.

This should be good. Lanny never says a word, and he's going to negotiate?

Lizzie noticed that her parents were also watching raptly.

Lanny stood there silently, listening to whoever was on the other end of the line. After a few minutes, he grinned and handed the phone back to Matt.

"Then we've got a deal," Matt said to the caller. "We'll see you tomorrow afternoon."

"That has got to be one of the strangest negotiations I've ever seen," Mr. McGuire murmured.

"But successful," Matt said as he attempted to butter his toast with his spoon. "Lanny just doubled our price."

Miranda waited until the Friday afternoon lunch crowd had thinned before she approached her aunt with Lizzie's request. Alejandra was in the kitchen, starting a sauce for that night's dinner.

Miranda stood nearby, waiting until her aunt had finished adding spices to the pot.

"*Tia*," Miranda began. "I need to ask you about a *tres leches* cake."

"*Tres leches?*" Alejandra said, smiling. "I haven't made one of those in ages. Maybe that's what I should add to the dessert menu. I think people would like it."

"Actually, I was wondering if you would bake one for someone else," Miranda said, and explained about Rosa, and Lizzie wanting to surprise her for her birthday. "Lizzie and I will pay for it," Miranda finished hurriedly. "We'll use money from our allowances."

To Miranda's surprise, her aunt bent forward and brushed the top of her head with a kiss. "That's good of you, *chica*, but I won't ask that this come out of your pocket. When is Rosa's birthday?"

"Next Wednesday."

"Tell you what," her aunt said. "Next week I'll bake three *tres leches* cakes, two for the restaurant and one for Rosa and the senior center."

Miranda gave her aunt a hug. "Thanks so much, *Tia*."

"And now," Alejandra said, "would you get clean vases from the dishwasher and put them on the tables for tonight? The florist came this morning and left the flowers in the refrigerator on the right. Ask Josh to help you."

"Got it," Miranda said. She crossed to the other side of the kitchen, where Josh was unloading the dishwasher.

"Hey," he said, giving Miranda a smile that somehow made her feel warm and happy inside. "What's up?"

"I've come to get the vases for the tables," Miranda explained. "Aunt Alejandra wants me to get flowers for them and put them out." She hesitated a moment before adding, "She said you could help me. If you want, that is."

"Sure," he said.

Together they removed the vases from the dishwasher and filled each one with cool water and a pinch of sugar to keep the flowers alive. Then they took the cut flowers from the fridge and began to arrange them in the vases. Miranda liked making the arrangements. It was fun to choose a selection of flowers for each vase and try to make each one beautiful.

Josh seemed totally absorbed in the task, too. They worked comfortably, side by side. Neither spoke for a while. Miranda couldn't help sneaking looks at Josh every so often. He was so cute.

Stop that! she told herself. After all, the reason she had suggested Josh apply for the dishwashing job was so she could find a way to get him and Lizzie together. Lizzie had seen him first, Miranda reminded herself, and Lizzie was the one with the major crush.

Miranda realized that she didn't really know anything about Josh, which made it hard to play matchmaker.

"So, Josh," she said. "What do you like to do? I mean, aside from skateboarding and washing dishes."

Josh seemed surprised by the question at first. "Um, I really like baseball," he said, smiling at her.

"Me, too!" Miranda said. "I love going to baseball games."

"We should take one in sometime," Josh suggested.

"Definitely," Miranda replied, and then stopped, her eyes wide with alarm.

"What's wrong?" Josh asked.

"Uh, nothing." Miranda busied herself selecting more flowers. But she knew exactly what she'd done. She'd agreed to a date—sort of—with Lizzie's new crush-boy. "It's just that I don't really know if I can go to a game with you," she explained. "I have to work at the restaurant a lot."

Josh frowned. "I thought you only worked three days a week, like me."

"I do," Miranda said, "but because I'm family, um—I'm always on call."

Josh grinned. "You make it sound like the ER. It's just a restaurant."

"Yes, but it's new, and you know how exacting my aunt is," Miranda went on. She knew she ought to stop talking before she said something completely stupid. She loaded a serving tray with vases and carried them into the dining room. Carefully, she began to set them on the tables.

This was going to be tricky, she realized. She still had no clear idea of how she was going to get Lizzie and Josh together. The only thing she knew for certain was that she was going to have to be very careful around Josh Russell. Because if she wasn't, she might find herself falling for him—hard!

* * *

Gordo went to a local pizza parlor for lunch on Thursday. He ate alone, using the time to write down questions he would ask in his interviews at the amusement park the next day. He started back to the *Chronicle* offices, ready to type them up.

The interns' office was empty, so he sat down at the computer and began typing.

That's when he noticed the magazine on the desk. It was *Fashion Forward,* one of the teen fashion zines that Lizzie and Miranda were always reading. He was about to toss the magazine in the trash. But then he realized it was open to an article entitled "How to Get the Hottie of Your Dreams to Notice You."

Gordo stopped typing his interview questions. He checked the magazine cover, but there was no address label. That meant it had been left there by Kate or Ingrid or Lorene.

The gears in Gordo's overactive imagination began to whir. First the bouquet—designed to be a message from a secret admirer—and now this article. Was it possible that they were both left here deliberately for *him* to find? Was it possible that *he* actually had a secret admirer? What if he, David "Gordo" Gordon, was the hottie?

CHAPTER NINE

"**M**orning," Lizzie said as she entered the auditorium, bright and early on Friday.

The curtains to the stage were open and Colin was kneeling beside some sort of metal box, a screwdriver in his hand. "Not now," he muttered without looking up.

"What's not now?" she asked.

He finally turned to look at her. "I can't deal with any questions now," he explained.

"The mechanism that moves the curtains broke and I have to fix it."

"Oh," Lizzie said. "So you don't want me to paint more scenery?" She felt a little disappointed, especially since she had dressed for the job in white painter's overalls, and sneakers that were already paint-splotched from working on a Christmas float. She had even tied a pink bandanna over her hair.

"Didn't I just tell you I didn't want any questions?" Colin snapped.

So much for Mr. Nice Guy.

"Excuse me, your highness," Lizzie said indignantly. "I came here to help. So it seems to me that if you're having trouble with the curtain, it would make sense to ask me to do something else."

Colin threw his hands up in the air and got to his feet. "Fine," he said. "The swing group will be here to rehearse in five minutes, and Sandra is going to want to go over all of the lighting cues. Why don't you run the lighting board?"

"Um . . . because I've never run a lighting board?" Lizzie replied.

"I'll show you." Colin jumped down from the stage and walked to a point about midway up in the rows, where the seats stopped and there was something that looked like a rectangular black box on a table.

"These are the footlights," Colin said, pressing a button. "You'll definitely want those on."

Lizzie smiled as the row of lights at the foot of the stage lit up, suddenly making the small auditorium feel like a real theater.

"And these dimmers control the spots." Colin pushed one of the switches, and the light on the stage grew brighter. "They're going to have two groups of four couples, which means you want a spot on each group." He began sliding switches around, quickly identifying them. Lizzie's eyes darted from the lighting board to the stage as she tried to memorize everything he was saying. "Okay," he finished. "I'm going back to work on the curtain. Just ask Sandra what kind of lights she wants."

"Right," Lizzie said. "No problem."

All I have to do is push a few buttons. How hard can that be?

Colin had no sooner returned to the stage than the auditorium door opened and the swing group came in.

"Hi, Lizzie," Sandra called out cheerfully. "I see you're working the lights today."

"It's my first time," Lizzie admitted, trying to sound confident.

As the dancers climbed onstage, Sandra brought Lizzie her laptop. A long extension cord connected it to the speaker system. "Since Colin's wrestling with the stage curtain, would you cue the music, as well?" Sandra asked.

"No problem," Lizzie said. That, at least, was easy.

The four couples arranged themselves in the wings of the stage and Lizzie turned on the footlights.

"Song one," Sandra called. "And can you give me a spot on each side of the stage?"

"I think so," Lizzie answered. She got the first song playing, and stared at the lighting board. Did the switch on the right control the right spot? She couldn't quite remember what Colin had said, but it seemed like a good guess. She hit the switch on the right and a light began circling the stage.

"Not a circle, dear," Sandra called. "Two spots, stage left and stage right."

"Sorry," Lizzie called back.

She pushed two more buttons. These were miraculously the right ones.

Lizzie started the song again. Sandra counted, "And five and six and seven and eight," and the couples began to dance onto the stage. In the middle of the song, Sandra called, "Lizzie, they just danced out of the lights. The spot has to follow them to the center of the stage."

"Definitely." Lizzie took a wild guess and

pressed two more switches. One group of dancers was suddenly bathed in bright green light, the other group in magenta. Confused by the colors, everyone lost the beat.

Frantically, Lizzie pressed another button. A strobe light began to flash, making the stage look as if it were in the middle of a magenta and green lightning storm.

"Turn that thing off!" Marcus yelled. "Flashing lights make me dizzy."

"Sorry," Lizzie murmured. She stared at the board. Which one controlled the strobe? She was beginning to panic. She pressed another button and a bright blue light was added to the mix.

No one will say it wasn't colorful.

Marcus sat down in the middle of the stage. "I'll get up as soon as that strobe stops," he said. "I think I'm nauseous."

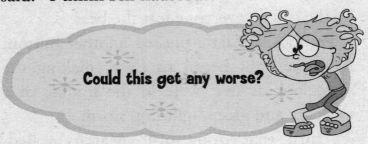

Could this get any worse?

Sandra groaned and hurried toward the lighting board just as Lizzie managed to find the strobe switch and shut it off.

"Lizzie, dear," Sandra said. "Why don't we save the lighting cues for another rehearsal?"

"That would be great," Lizzie said. The couples danced for another half hour or so, but everyone was a little off. The strobe had left Grace with a headache, and Marcus was still dizzy.

Seconds after the swing group shuffled out

of the auditorium, the curtain swept across the stage. Colin emerged from behind it. "It's fixed," he said.

"That's just terrific." Lizzie's temper was starting to boil. "In the meantime, I almost drove the seniors crazy. I used the wrong color lights, and everyone lost the beat. And poor Marcus got so dizzy from the strobes that he had to sit down. Sandra had to ask me to stop working the board. It was awful!"

"I'm sorry," Colin said. "It wasn't fair to ask you to run the board without giving you a chance to practice."

Wait a minute. Now he gets all reasonable? I was just warming up for a good fight.

"You're right," she said, trying to hold on to her indignation. "You should have given me a chance to practice—and a much better explanation. And a chart—with labels and things."

"Right," Colin said, grinning. "Next time a chart. With labels."

Lizzie sniffed, not sure she should stop being mad at him.

"And I'm sorry I snapped at you, and if I've been hard to work with," he added, "it's just that this is my first real, paying job. The center took a big chance, hiring someone so young to be their entire stage crew. I just don't want to mess up. I've been so focused on being perfect that I think I've been kind of a jerk."

"Yeah, you could say so," Lizzie agreed. Then something he said sunk in. "Wait, you mean you're not a volunteer like the rest of us?"

Colin shook his head. "Nope, I'm here five

days a week, and I'm responsible for the stage, the lighting and sound, the sets, the whole thing."

"Wow," Lizzie said. "That's a pretty big job to do all by yourself."

"Yeah," Colin agreed. "But it's no excuse for the way I've been acting."

He stepped forward. "Thanks for being such a good sport about it." He gazed at her, and for a moment, Lizzie thought he might kiss her. The thought made her very nervous.

My heart is beating so loudly and quickly. And loudly.

"Sure, no problem," she blurted, trying to calm herself down. "So how did you learn to do all this theater stuff, anyway?"

Colin took a step back. "My dad runs the Shakespeare Theater downtown, so I've spent a lot of time backstage." He shrugged. "By the time I was eight, I knew how to run lighting and sound boards."

"I don't know how to do either one," Lizzie confessed. "But I'm a very talented shopper."

Colin smiled at her. "Do you think your talents might include painting some more scenery?"

"Anything but running the lights!" Lizzie told him, relieved to have something to do. Why had she thought Colin would kiss her? Anyway, what did it matter? It was Josh she liked. And Ethan, of course.

Lizzie shifted her weight on the amusement-park bench. It was Saturday afternoon, the sun was beating down, and she was wedged between Gordo and Miranda. Ingrid sat on the other side of Gordo, and Josh sat on the other side of Miranda.

Once again, the seating arrangements could be better.

They were all watching three bears with bright blue fur dance and sing about vegetables. A row of little kids sat on the bench in front of them, clapping and singing along.

"Tell me again why we're doing this," Lizzie whispered to Gordo.

"Because I'm interviewing the bears about their summer jobs," Gordo whispered back.

Lizzie was trying not to think about the fact that aside from a muttered, "hey," Josh hadn't said a word to her. Miranda had called that morning and said she was inviting Josh, so he and Lizzie could stop feeling weird about the cat scene at the senior center.

Progress report?
Miranda's plan is not working.

The bears finished their routine, and Gordo and Ingrid went up to the stage to interview them.

"Want to go on some rides?" Miranda asked Lizzie and Josh.

"Sure," Lizzie said. "It's hot out. Let's go on the log flume."

"Listen, Josh," Miranda said as they stood on line for the ride. "I need to tell you something. When I went on and on about it being fine to bring pets to the senior center, I didn't know what I was talking about."

"Really?" Josh said sarcastically.

"And I should have told you there's a resident cat," Lizzie added. "I shouldn't have let Miranda go on like that."

"No kidding." Josh gave them both a reluctant smile. "Listen, it all worked out. Precious is fine, and my grandmother calmed down."

The three of them had a fine time on the ride after that, and by the time they got off—damp but laughing—Lizzie was feeling much better about things.

Until she heard an awful, but familiar, scratching sound. "Oh, no," she moaned. "It's the rodent!"

Does he follow me around on purpose?

"He's really serious about this music thing, isn't he?" Gordo said, coming up to join them.

"Who is that kid?" asked Ingrid, a few steps behind Gordo.

Lizzie shut her eyes. "My pesky little brother," she murmured.

"I hate to tell you this," Ingrid said, "but your pesky little brother's got a following."

Lizzie opened her eyes. Ingrid was right. A crowd was gathering in front of Lanny and Matt's makeshift stage. And they were all dancing to Matt's dreadful music.

Josh shrugged. "If you can't beat 'em, might as well join 'em." He moved into the crowd and started dancing.

"Why not?" Miranda said with a laugh, and went to join him.

Lizzie, though, couldn't do it. Not to Matt's music. So while Ingrid snapped photos, Lizzie stood with Gordo and watched Miranda and Josh rock out.

"You know what?" Gordo said. "They make a really cute couple."

Lizzie rested her elbow on his shoulder and sighed. "I was thinking exactly the same thing," she said.

CHAPTER TEN

On Wednesday afternoon Lizzie found herself waiting nervously in the lounge. The seniors were all gathered there because Ada had told them she had an announcement.

Just then, Miranda and Josh came in, carrying a large box.

For once, something I planned is going to work!

"We have a special delivery for Ms. Rosa Martinez," Miranda announced.

Rosa was sitting at one of the tables, working on some knitting. "She's right here," Lizzie said, relieved.

Miranda and Josh set the box on the table in front of Rosa, and Lizzie lifted the lid, revealing a long sheet cake covered in creamy white icing.

Rosa set down her knitting with a gasp. "Is it really a *tres leches* cake?"

"It is," Lizzie told her. "Miranda's aunt Alejandra baked it specially for you. Happy birthday, Rosa!"

Then everyone sang "Happy Birthday."

"Oh, my," Rosa said softly.

Lizzie brought over a stack of paper plates and forks and a cake knife, and began to cut the cake. She gave the first piece to Rosa, while Jasmine, Miranda, and Josh served coffee and iced tea.

Lizzie watched anxiously as Rosa took the first bite. "Is it okay?" Lizzie asked.

"Okay?" Rosa echoed. "It's the best *tres leches* I've ever eaten." She shook her head, laughing. "I'm never going to be able to tell my sister about this. Thank you, Lizzie. You've made me very happy."

"You're totally welcome," Lizzie said.

Okay, maybe my mom was right. Volunteer work *does* feel good.

Unfortunately, the warm fuzzies didn't last. Lizzie couldn't help noticing that while Josh and Miranda were serving the drinks, they kept looking at each other. Were they just sort of checking in? Or were they all-out crushing on each other?

"Rosa, we have one more surprise for you," Ada announced. "We know you love Elvis's music, so—" She held her arm out, the door to the lounge opened, and two very short Elvises, carrying a turntable and a few vinyl records, trotted into the lounge.

Lizzie felt her jaw drop in horror. "Not again!" she muttered. Even Elvis wigs and rhinestone-studded jumpsuits couldn't disguise Matt and Lanny.

Does he have a tracking device?

She felt Miranda grasp her arm. "Steady, Lizzie," she murmured. "They'll sing a few songs and it will all be over."

Ada smiled at Lizzie. "You left your brother's

cards on the table, so I called. Matt told me they could do Elvis."

"Can we ever!" Matt said.

Lanny plugged in the turntable, Matt put on a record of Elvis's greatest hits, and the two little Elvi, as Lizzie had started to think of them, did some of the weirdest lip-synching ever.

Josh looked confused. "Is this supposed to be karaoke?" he asked.

"Don't ask me," Lizzie said.

"They're jumping around pretty good," Miranda observed.

Somehow both Matt and Lanny had gotten some of the King's moves down. They even ended one song by sliding on their knees.

The seniors loved it. They were all standing up, applauding. For the first time, Marcus and Clarice even seemed to be getting along. And Rosa, who was up on her feet dancing, looked happier than Lizzie had ever seen her.

Matt and Lanny began another song. Lizzie surrendered and sat down to watch. Miranda and Josh were watching too, and Lizzie couldn't help but notice how close together they were. Their shoulders were touching.

I know it's a horrible thought, but I have to ask: is Miranda trying to steal Josh?

Later that afternoon, after everyone had gone, Lizzie stayed to help clean up. "Your party was quite the success," Ada told her.

"I think Rosa really enjoyed it," Lizzie agreed. "And I have to admit—hiring my brother was actually a good idea."

Ada nodded as she collected paper plates. "Yes, I had no idea that Clarice and Marcus were both Elvis fans. Finally, we found some-thing they can agree on! It's strange how things work out. Speaking of which—" She gave Lizzie a shrewd look. "You shouldn't waste your time wanting what you can't have."

"What does that mean?" Lizzie asked.

But the phone rang, and Ada went to pick it up, saying, "Oh, I think you'll figure it out."

That evening, after dinner, Lizzie called Miranda. She thanked her for bringing the cake and then told her what Ada had said.

"I think I know what she was talking about," Lizzie confessed. "I think she meant Josh, that he isn't for me."

"That's ridiculous!" Miranda said indig-nantly. "Ada doesn't know Josh and she barely knows you. But I know you both, and I know you're perfect for each other. Oh, I just had an amazing brainstorm!"

Uh-oh. She has that dangerous gleam in her eye again, I can tell.

"Tomorrow, you and Josh are going to come to the restaurant—not the taco bar," Miranda declared. "I am going to get you two together for the most romantic dinner ever."

So much for my theory that Miranda is trying to steal Josh.

"Slow down," Lizzie said. "How do you know Josh would even agree to have a romantic dinner with me?"

"He's not going to know!" Miranda

explained. "I'll ask if he can come to the restaurant to help out. When he shows, I'll tell him it's for a special friends' dinner. It will start with the three of us, but I'll have Aunt Alejandra call me into the kitchen for some fake emergency. And then it will just be you and Josh!"

Lizzie thought it over. On one hand, she liked Josh and wanted to get to know him. On the other hand, something in her gut told her Ada was right. On the third hand—a romantic dinner with Josh sounded dreamy.

On the third hand? Could this be the problem with my thought process?

"Okay, I guess," she agreed.

"Perfecto!" Miranda said. "Be at the restaurant tomorrow at four thirty."

CHAPTER ELEVEN

On Thursday morning, Gordo was headed to work for an editorial meeting. He crossed the plaza in front of the *Chronicle* building and was about to open one of the big glass doors when he stopped. Did I really just see that? he wondered.

I couldn't have, he told himself. It had to be my imagination.

Still, he couldn't resist turning around and

walking back to the fountain in the center of the plaza.

Gordo lifted his shades to be sure. Nope, it wasn't his imagination. Kate had gotten Larry Tudgeman to do a fashion makeover, and they were doing a photo shoot.

Tudge, dressed weirdly like Ethan Craft—complete with a beaded choker—was standing in front of the fountain. Claire, who was one of Kate's evil crew, was holding a battery-operated fan in front of his face, so that his hair blew back toward the geysering water. Ingrid was crouched a short distance away, focusing her camera on Tudge. And Kate was directing the whole operation.

"Larry, it looks like the water is spouting out of your head," Kate complained. "I want your gaze more over your left shoulder."

Tudgeman tried to turn his head to the left,

and winced. "I can't. This choker is too tight. It's choking me. And the fountain is spraying me. I'm wet and cold!"

"Glamour is never easy," Kate told him. "All models suffer for their art."

"But I'm not a model!" Tudge protested.

Kate frowned at him. "Hold on, you're too pale." She fished a silvery jar from her purse and smeared some blush on his cheeks.

"He looks completely miserable," said a sympathetic voice.

Gordo turned to see Lorene standing beside him. "Oh, it's more than looks," he assured her. "Tudge is totally miserable."

"We've got to do something," Lorene said.

"And soon," Gordo agreed.

And then he got an idea. "I'm going to need your help," he told Lorene, and began whispering his plan.

Kate was so busy bossing everyone around

that she never noticed Lorene making her way to the edge of the fountain, opposite Tudgeman.

Lorene took a deep breath and gave a bloodcurdling shriek as she pointed toward the water. Everyone around the fountain instantly stopped what they were doing and looked at Lorene.

"L-look! It-it's huge!" Lorene's hand was shaking and she sounded completely terrified. "It's sw-swimming!"

Tudge looked, Claire and Ingrid looked, and even Kate came up to see what was in the water.

That was the moment Gordo was waiting for. He darted up behind Kate and pushed. As Kate landed in the fountain with a splash, Gordo grabbed Tudge by the arm and they made their escape.

A few minutes later, Gordo and Tudge met

up with Lorene at the back entrance to the building.

"That was brilliant acting!" Gordo told Lorene. "You could audition for a horror flick."

Lorene grinned. "I was convincing, wasn't I?" she asked.

"Totally!" Tudgeman pulled off the beaded choker. "I expected to see an escaped alligator in there." He gave Gordo a worried glance. "Did you hear Kate shrieking? That was serious Darth Vader rage. She's never going to forgive us for this."

Gordo shrugged. "She had it coming."

"Come on." Lorene looped an arm through each of theirs. "We'd better get upstairs before Jerome starts his meeting."

As they started toward the elevators, Gordo again wondered if he had a secret admirer. And he thought that if he did and it turned out to be Lorene, he really wouldn't mind.

* * *

Lizzie carried a platter of appetizers out of Alejandra's kitchen to the dining room, where Miranda was setting a table covered with a white cloth. There was already a vase of flowers on the table and a candle was lit.

"Put the platter down here," Miranda said, readjusting the three place settings. "Do you think it looks okay?"

"More than okay," Lizzie said.

Is it possible for something to look *too* romantic?

"It's going to be perfect for you and Josh," Miranda assured her.

Miranda was dressed in low-rise jeans and a red top with beaded trim. Lizzie thought she looked perfect—totally casual and comfortable, but also really pretty. In contrast, Lizzie felt stuffy and overdressed. She was wearing a white blouse with a ruffled collar, and ruffles down the front over a knee-length black skirt with a ruffled hem.

"Miranda, I need to go home and change," Lizzie said nervously.

Miranda glanced at her watch. "You can't! It's almost four thirty. Josh is going to be here any minute!"

"Well, do you have something less fussy I can put on?"

Miranda shook her head. "Don't worry. You look great."

I look like I'm going to give a speech to the Ruffle Society of America.

"He's here," Miranda whispered as the bell over the front door rang.

Lizzie, who'd had butterflies in her stomach before, now felt as if there were grasshoppers jumping around in there.

Josh was dressed for work in jeans and a faded blue T-shirt. As usual, he looked totally amazing.

He saw Miranda and his eyes lit up. "Hey," he said. "You look—" He saw Lizzie and stopped. "Oh, hi, Lizzie," he said, and turned back to Miranda. "So what's going on that you needed me to come in on my day off?"

"Actually, that was a lie," Miranda said quickly. "My aunt's letting me give a special dinner here tonight for friends, and I wanted to surprise you."

"Cool," Josh said, and the three of them sat down at the table.

"So have some appetizers, everybody,"

Miranda said, passing the platter around.

Josh helped himself to a few empanadas, little golden pockets of piecrust filled with meats, vegetables, and cheese. "These are outrageous," he said.

Lizzie took one, too. But she had no appetite. The grasshoppers in her stomach started doing jumping jacks as Josh's eyes came to rest on her. "Was I supposed to get dressed up?" he asked uneasily.

"Oh, no," Miranda said at once. "Lizzie just likes fancy clothes. She has sort of—a formal streak!"

"Not usually," Lizzie corrected her. "Just once in a while. So," she said, desperate to change the subject, "what did you think of our amusement park?"

"I liked the blue bears," Josh said with a grin. "The rides were pretty standard, though. Like the stuff we have back home."

"What about the skate park?" Miranda asked. "Is that like what you have in San Francisco?"

"Actually, Kirkland is something special," Josh told them. "I've never been in such a radical skate park. I was telling my grandmother, it's a perfect design. They found a way to give you room for just about every possible move."

"And what did your grandmother say?" Lizzie thought it was pretty charming that Josh would talk about skateboarding with his grandmother.

Josh laughed. "She didn't know what I was talking about. So a couple of times a week now she walks Precious over to Kirkland and watches me. She's becoming a fan. I've almost got her using the lingo."

"Miranda!" Alejandra appeared from the kitchen, looking harried. She smiled briefly at Lizzie and Josh. "I need help in the kitchen, *chica.* Can you give me a few minutes?"

Josh got to his feet at once. "Can I help?"

"No, sit," Alejandra told him. "Tonight, you're my guest. I'll have Hector bring out the main course."

Miranda disappeared into the kitchen with her aunt, leaving Josh and Lizzie alone. Suddenly, the conversation, which had felt so light and easy a moment ago, came to a grinding halt.

It's so quiet and awkward.
And quiet.

Josh helped himself to another appetizer, and Lizzie tried to think of something to say.

For some reason she thought of Jasmine, who was always so interested in Zeke's job.

Obviously, she had to figure out what Josh was into.

"Do you have any hobbies?" she asked. "Other than skateboarding, I mean."

Hobbies? Who under the age of thirty has hobbies?

"Not really," Josh said.

Hector brought out a platter of chicken mole and basket of warm corn tortillas. "Man, I've been wanting to try this mole since the first day I worked here," Josh said, digging in.

Lizzie took a bite of the chicken covered in rich, chocolaty sauce, but she still had no appetite. She wished Miranda would come back to the table.

"Do you like sports?" she asked, feeling a little desperate.

Josh nodded. "Baseball."

"Me, too," Lizzie said weakly.

The truth? Every time I try to watch a baseball game, I fall asleep.

"What do you think of the A's this year?" Josh asked.

"The A's?" Lizzie wasn't sure of whether that was the name of a team or perhaps a grade—like maybe there were A teams and B teams. She decided it was safest to answer with a joke. "They're uh—A-okay!"

Josh looked at her quizzically. "They've lost fifteen games in a row," he told her. He suddenly swiveled toward the front of the restaurant. "What was that noise?"

Lizzie peered across the courtyard, where she could see that about a dozen teenage boys had come in. They were all crowded around the taco bar. One of them knocked over a smoothie.

Josh turned. "I'd better clean that up," he said, and headed into the kitchen.

Cleaning had not been on Lizzie's agenda, but she felt she ought to volunteer, too. "I'll sponge down the bar," she offered.

Josh looked back. "That's okay, I've got it," he called.

Although Lizzie stayed for a bit, the dinner seemed to be over. In the end, she wound up going home.

Maybe it's time to face facts. Josh Russell would rather mop a floor than have dinner with me!

CHAPTER TWELVE

Lizzie was sprawled across her bed, feeling sorry for herself, when she heard a knock at the door.

Hey, I deserve at least one evening of self-pity.

Lizzie opened the bedroom door and saw Miranda and Gordo. "Come on in," she said bleakly. "It's officially over. I'm giving up on Josh."

"You can't do that!" Miranda said.

"Why can't she?" Gordo wondered.

"Because I know Josh likes her," Miranda insisted.

Lizzie plopped down on the bed again. "Honestly, Miranda, it's hopeless. He told me he liked baseball, and I lied and said I did, too, and then I didn't know what the A's were. He thinks I'm an idiot and couldn't wait to get away from me."

"He doesn't think you're an idiot," Miranda said loyally.

"If he does, he's missing out big-time," Gordo added.

Yeah, he'd be missing more insightful comments on baseball.

"But could we change the subject for a minute to my romantic life?" Gordo asked. "Or *potential* romantic life," he added more accurately. "Look at what I found today on the computer I share with the other interns." He handed them each a three-page printout.

Lizzie skimmed it quickly. It was about a girl who was crushing madly on a boy, but the boy didn't know it. "Is this fiction?" she asked.

"That's what I'm wondering," Gordo admitted. "It's written like a short story, but I've had other hints that I might have a secret admirer, so . . . do you think that's what this story is about? Was I meant to find it—like some kind of secret message? Or am I totally deluded?"

Gordo has a secret admirer? Huh.

Miranda, who was still reading the story, looked up and said, "I don't know, Gordo. Anything's possible."

Lizzie found it difficult to be at the senior center on Friday morning. She was still blue about Josh. And everyone in the lounge that morning looked so happy. Clarice and Marcus were definitely clicking, she noticed.

Even seventy-year-olds are connecting! What's wrong with me?

Lizzie went to get some orange juice. Then she looked at her watch and gasped. The morning's swing rehearsal had just started and she was supposed to work the music for Sandra.

Lizzie raced for the auditorium. She found Sandra and the dancers already on the stage. Colin was adjusting something on the lighting board.

"There you are, Lizzie," Sandra said. "Thank goodness, you're not sick, too."

"Who's sick?" Lizzie asked as she ran up to the stage and positioned herself near Sandra's laptop.

"Grace and Harry just phoned in," Sandra explained. "They've got a nasty summer flu. Both of them are down with it."

"That's awful," Lizzie said. She felt badly for Grace and Harry, of course. But she also felt badly for Sandra. Grace and Harry were the best dancers in the group.

Sandra looked at the remaining dancers and shook her head. "Here I am with choreography for four couples and I've only got three to work with. Well, we'll just have to adapt.

"Okay, everybody, let's form a triangle. Clarice and Marcus, you'll be front and center. Lizzie, cue song one, please."

It turned out to be the most frustrating rehearsal Lizzie had seen. The three couples tried hard to learn the new formations, but everything seemed off balance. Sandra had Lizzie start the songs again and again, because the dancers couldn't get through them without making a million mistakes.

"Okay, Lizzie, please turn off the music. Dancers, take a break," Sandra called. Lizzie noticed then that Ada had come into the auditorium and was sitting beside Sandra. The two women conferred quietly for a moment.

Sandra stood up and faced Colin, who was bent over the lighting board. "Could you help me out here?" she said simply.

This is interesting, Lizzie thought. Sandra

must be pretty desperate if she's asking the theater techie to substitute for one of her dancers.

Colin's head snapped up, and Lizzie saw that his mouth was drawn in a tense line. "I didn't sign on to dance," he said. "My job is strictly behind the scenes."

"Please," Ada said. "Just for this rehearsal."

Moving slowly and rather stiffly, Colin walked up onstage.

"You'll need a partner," Sandra said in a distracted tone. "Lizzie, would you mind?"

Me, dance?
In front of people???

"Me?" Lizzie asked, aghast. "I can't."

"Of course you can, dear," Ada told her.

"You don't understand," Lizzie insisted, her

panic rising. "I am a complete klutz. I trip over my own feet all the time. I can't partner dance! I don't know any of the steps!"

"It's just practice," Sandra said. "Besides, the boy leads. All you have to do is follow."

"Just try it," Ada said in her most soothing tone. "I'll cue the music."

Lizzie realized she had no choice. She managed to get up onstage without falling. Colin held his hands out to her. He looked every bit as uncomfortable as Lizzie felt.

"Everyone, your original places. Ada, song one," Sandra called. The intro to the song began, and Sandra counted aloud. "And five and six and seven and eight!"

And then Lizzie and Colin were moving across the stage, more or less keeping up with the other couples. Lizzie had no idea of what her feet were supposed to be doing. Strangely, Colin's feet seemed to know. She kept her head down and tried to mimic what he was doing.

"Ow!" he said, as her foot came down on his toe.

Lizzie winced. "Sorry."

"Swing out and triple-step," Sandra said.

"Whatever that means," Lizzie mumbled. She looked up for a moment and stepped on Colin's foot again.

Colin winced, but kept on dancing. The important thing seemed to be that he kept them in the right place onstage, so that the other couples were no longer getting confused. Thanks to Colin, they managed to move forward, backward, and to the sides when they were supposed to. But when he spun her into a turn at the end, Lizzie got dizzy and fell.

"Are you all right?" Colin asked, helping her to her feet.

Lizzie nodded, thoroughly embarrassed.

Why couldn't I haven't gotten the "graceful" gene?

"I think that's enough of rehearsal for today," Sandra announced.

"Yeah, I'd have to agree with that," Lizzie said, releasing her death grip on Colin's hand.

Colin turned and started backstage. "Wait a minute," Lizzie said, chasing after him. "How did you know all those steps?"

"I've been watching the rehearsals every day," he replied with a scowl. "Haven't you?"

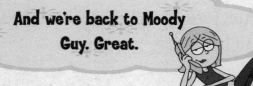

And we're back to Moody Guy. Great.

CHAPTER THIRTEEN

Later that day, Lizzie returned to the lounge after helping out in a water aerobics class. At least she'd gotten in a swim, and she felt cool and refreshed. It was four o'clock, and the seniors were all leaving.

Lizzie was getting ready to leave, when Ada called her over.

"Grace phoned me," Ada explained. "She and Harry just got home from the doctor. He told them they're going to need at least a week of rest. That means they won't be dancing in the show next Friday night."

"That's awful," Lizzie said. "Sandra's going to be so disappointed."

"Yes, I've talked to Sandra, too," Ada said. "She'd like you and Colin to fill in for them."

There has never been a worse idea in the world!

"But I was awful," Lizzie protested.

"Well, there's room for improvement," Ada replied, "but you have a full week to practice."

A week? Were we at the same rehearsal?

"That's not enough," Lizzie said, dread filling her chest.

Ada looked thoughtful. "I'm sure something can be worked out. Perhaps Sandra can simplify the steps for you."

Lizzie was now firmly in the grip of a panic attack. "Ada, I like working here, and I've done everything you've asked. But please, please, please don't ask me to dance! Especially up onstage in front of everyone. It will be a disaster." A moment of inspiration struck. "Why can't Jasmine do it? She's tall and willowy, like a dancer. She'll look much better with Colin."

Ada laughed. "I assure you it wouldn't work unless Jasmine could dance with her cell phone. I'm lucky when I can get that girl to simply sit down and talk to the seniors. Though she is getting better."

Lizzie shut her eyes. "I can't," she said in a small voice.

"Yes, you can," Ada said, her voice strong and sure. "I've been watching you, Lizzie McGuire, and I'm convinced you can do anything when you set your mind to it."

Lizzie opened one suspicious eye. "What makes you so sure?"

"Let's just say I've studied people all my life," Ada answered. "Before I took this job, I spent a lot of time figuring out what would and wouldn't work for them."

Then you should have figured out that I can't dance!

"You were a scientist?" Lizzie asked, realizing she knew nothing about Ada.

"Not exactly," Ada said. "But please trust me on this. You'll dance in the performance next Friday, and you'll do a wonderful job. I don't have a single doubt. Here." She handed Lizzie a card with a phone number scrawled on it. "That's the number for Sandra's dance studio. Call her this weekend and tell her your size, so she can get you a costume."

"A costume?" The word made Lizzie's blood run cold. This couldn't really be happening.

She had stopped arguing, though she wasn't sure why.

Then as she walked out of the senior center, she understood. Ada really did believe in her, and Lizzie didn't want to let her down.

Lizzie set off for home in a daze. She knew she needed a plan.

Maybe I can run away to a nice beach in the Caribbean. . . .

"Lizzie, can I talk to you for a minute?"

Lizzie turned to see Colin. He was sitting on a bench outside the community center. "I was waiting for you," he admitted, getting to his feet. "Did you hear about Grace and Harry?"

Lizzie nodded. "Ada told me. She sort of convinced me to dance next Friday night, but it's a terrible idea. I can't do it." Lizzie gave him a rueful smile. "When you called my name, I was making plans to run away to the Caribbean."

Colin began to walk with her. "The Caribbean sounds good," he said. "But I don't think I can afford the flight."

"I've got all of twenty-eight dollars saved," Lizzie admitted.

He sighed. "I don't think we can get out of it. Not without quitting our summer jobs entirely. And I don't want to quit mine."

"I don't want to quit, either," Lizzie said, a little surprised to realize this was true.

"Well, then maybe we should just do the best we can," Colin said. "It would help—a lot—if we could practice. Any chance you'd be up for practicing right now?"

Lizzie considered this. "As long as I'm home for dinner by six, I guess it's okay." She looked around. They were standing on a street corner, with traffic all around them. "Maybe we should go back to the HCC. We might be able to get into that room with the mirrored wall."

"I have a better idea," Colin said. "Come on, this place isn't far, and no one will be there to watch us flub."

Lizzie followed Colin for three blocks until he came to the Sandra Wolcott Dance Studio. Colin reached into his pocket, pulled out a key ring, and unlocked the door.

"Wait a minute," Lizzie said. "Sandra gave you the key to her studio?"

"Yeah," Colin replied, "when I was six." He studied Lizzie's uncomprehending expression for a moment. "You don't know, do you?" he asked softly.

"Know what?"

Colin shrugged. "Sandra's my mother."

"B-but she's Sandra Wolcott, and you're Colin Lang."

"Wolcott is the name she had before she married, when she was competing and winning dance contests. My dad's name is Lang."

"Oh," Lizzie said. Something else was occurring to her. "So that means you've had experience dancing."

"Pretty much since I could walk," Colin told her. "I was entered in my first ballroom competition when I was five." He opened the door and stepped inside. "Come on, we've only got an hour before people start to show for the evening classes."

Lizzie followed him into a big, airy studio, where he switched on the lights and put a disk in a CD player.

"Let's start with a basic triple step," Colin said. "Then I'll show you how to a do a rock step, a swing out, and a swivel. We'll work up to the underarm pass into a spin."

Lizzie must have had an alarmed expression on her face, because Colin laughed. "Look, I promise I'll break it down and make it simple," he said. "Trust me, I've had a lot of practice at this."

Lizzie and Colin faced the mirrors. "A triple step is just three steps," he explained. "First, we're going to triple-step in place. Listen to the music and come in on one. And five, six, seven, eight . . . one, two, three. One, two, three."

Colin moved slowly, and Lizzie found that it wasn't hard to follow, even when he did the triple step to the front and sides and back.

"Good," Colin said. "Now triple-step and turn to your right."

Lizzie, to her delight, found she could do this too without falling.

"And triple-step, triple-step, rock-step," Colin said, demonstrating.

Concentrating hard, her eyes going from Colin's feet to her own reflection, Lizzie was able to imitate his moves. Working this way, Colin was able to teach her some individual steps, which they put together in a pattern.

"Okay, you've got the pattern," Colin said. "Want to try as partners?"

With you—a professional dancer?

Lizzie shook her head. "Not unless you want me to step on your feet again."

"I'll risk it," Colin told her, and something in the way he was smiling at her melted away her fear.

Colin put one hand on the small of Lizzie's back. "Put your right hand on my shoulder," he told her.

Lizzie did, moving closer to him. And she felt her heart begin to race.

Colin gazed into her eyes and brushed a loose strand of hair back from her face.

He cleared his throat. "Okay, triple-step toward me. Let yourself feel the music and triple-step back, then forward again."

Lizzie snapped back into focus. All at once they were dancing the pattern in perfect time to the music. Lizzie couldn't quite believe it. She kept dancing until she started to laugh.

"What's so funny?" Colin asked.

"It's fun," she told him, as he spun her under one arm.

"That's the way it should be," he told her with a smile. He released her hand and shut off the music. "Why don't we leave it there for today? We'll work on it again next time."

Lizzie was almost disappointed that the lesson was over, but she saw people coming toward the studio for their evening classes.

"Thanks, Colin," she said as she left.

"You're totally welcome," he told her.

Lizzie set off for home, her mind on Colin.

I was actually dancing! With Colin! And he was a dream. . . .

* * *

At home, Gordo had just advanced a level in the computer game he'd been playing for the last week—he now had the keys to the kingdom and to the underworld. Still, it was a fairly depressing thing to be doing on a Friday night. So he was surprised, happy, and a little relieved when the phone rang and it was Lorene.

"What's up?" he asked.

"I need more advice about Hypothetical Guy," she told him. "What if I've sent what I think are some pretty obvious messages, and he still doesn't get it?"

Gordo thought about the bouquet, the magazine article, and the short story he'd found on the interns' computer. "What kind of messages?" he asked. "I mean, how obvious were they?"

Lorene was silent for a moment before

saying, "Well, they were kind of disguised. But really, anyone who wasn't totally dense could figure it out."

"So you think this guy is dense?" Gordo asked, feeling a little defensive. That was ridiculous, he knew. Maybe Lorene wasn't even talking about him.

"Actually, I think Hypothetical Guy is supersmart," Lorene admitted. "He's just dense when it comes to this romance thing. I think maybe because he isn't your typical hottie, he hasn't had that much experience with crushes."

"That all fits," Gordo said. It did sound like him.

"So what do I do?" Lorene wanted to know.

"Um." Gordo thought. If he was Hypothetical Guy, how would he want Lorene to let him know? "You could be direct and just talk to him."

"I can't," Lorene said. "If he tells me he's not interested, I'll feel like a fool and never be able to look at him again. And we're sort of in this situation where we have to see each other a lot. It just wouldn't be cool."

The *Chronicle*, Gordo thought. They had to see each other nearly every day. Lorene *must* be talking about him.

"Well," Gordo said, "if he's so smart, he's probably noticed at least a few of these clues, and he's probably curious. I'd say, send him a few more. Build some intrigue so he has to wonder about you."

Lorene gave an uncomfortable cough. "Listen, there's another reason I called," she went on. "Tomorrow afternoon I'm going to the Odeon. They're showing *Strike Up the Band*. It's an old Judy Garland–Mickey Rooney musical. When it was made in 1940, it was a teen movie, and I thought it would be fun to do a column contrasting it with today's teen movies. Do you want to go?"

"Um, sure," Gordo said.

"Great, the movie's at three. Meet you inside?"

"I'll be there," Gordo said.

As he hung up the phone, a new and courageous idea occurred to him. Maybe *he* should ask Lorene if he was Hypothetical Guy.

CHAPTER FOURTEEN

Lizzie slept late on Saturday morning. She'd just opened her eyes when the phone rang. She checked the clock. It was ten thirty. She picked up the phone. "Hello," she said.

"Lizzie, it's Colin."

Lizzie was instantly wide-awake.

A boy is calling me!

"I was calling to see if you wanted to go to a movie this afternoon," he said. "The Odeon has a three o'clock showing of *Strike Up the Band*. It's one of those old Judy Garland–Mickey Rooney movies."

"Why that movie?" Lizzie asked, curious.

"Because it doesn't come around very often, and Busby Berkeley directed it, which means it has some amazing dancing, including some swing. I mean, it's kind of corny, but totally worth it for the dancing and singing."

"Cool," Lizzie said.

"Why don't we meet outside the theater at two thirty? That will give us plenty of time to buy tickets and get some ice cream at the place next door."

"See you then," Lizzie agreed. She hung up in a daze and began to walk down the hall.

Am I dreaming, or did Colin Lang just ask me out on a date?

* * *

Lizzie was at the Odeon at two thirty sharp. It was an older movie theater, with just one screen, that showed a weird and wonderful mix of films. It was the place to go when you were in the mood for something unusual.

Colin was waiting for her, holding two tickets. "We lucked out," he told her. "They're also showing a short called *The Big Apple*, which has some of the most famous Lindy Hop dancers ever."

They went into the ice cream parlor next door and snagged a booth. Colin ordered a mocha-chocolate-coconut concoction, and Lizzie went for the banana split.

The banana almost makes it
health food.

"I didn't realize you were so into dancing," she said as they waited for their orders.

"I'm not nearly as into it as my mom," he explained. "I bailed on the competitions last year. I sort of feel like, as a dancer, I've retired."

"Retired, huh? Then you must love working with the seniors," Lizzie teased. Then she grew serious. "Why did you stop competing?"

"Because I realized that dancing wasn't fun for me anymore. It was all this pressure to be perfect, to be better than everyone else. One day I just woke up and knew I didn't like that part of it and didn't want to do it anymore."

"Is that why you were upset when you got drafted into Talent Night?"

Colin grinned as their ice cream was set down on the table. "I thought I was off the hook, that I'd never have to perform again. Leave it to my mother to find a way to rope me into it."

"At least you know how to dance," Lizzie said. "I barely can do a triple step." She looked up at him and saw sympathy in his dark eyes. She took a deep breath. "Moment of truth," she said. "I'm going to be a disaster on Friday night."

"You're not," he said firmly. "We're going to practice this week, and you'll be fine."

"Don't lie," Lizzie said.

"I'm not." Colin squeezed her hand for just a moment, and what he said next sent a warm feeling straight into Lizzie's heart. "I think you and I are going to be great together."

* * *

The coming attractions were almost over when Lizzie and Colin settled into their seats. Lizzie stole a glance Colin. In the flickering light of the screen, he looked handsome. He was, Lizzie realized, a complete and total hottie. Just in a different way than either Ethan or Josh.

Lizzie turned her eyes to the screen as the scratchy old short began. Big band music came through the speakers, and Colin took her hand. Lizzie felt his fingers interlace with hers, warm and strong. And then she felt something else—the hand that held hers moving ever so slightly in perfect time to the music. Lizzie let her hand move with his. She felt a little thrill as she realized that even sitting in a movie theater, somehow it seemed as if the two of them were dancing together.

The short wasn't like anything she'd ever seen. It took place in some sort of ballroom, where there was a huge circle of dancers. A caller would call out steps and then couples would go into the middle of the circle and do amazing acrobatic dances, almost like they were competing.

"That's the Savoy Ballroom and the dance is what's called the Big Apple," Colin whispered to her. "It was really popular in New York in the 1930s. The guy doing the calling is Frankie Manning, one of the most famous swing dancers ever. He's the one who added all the lifts and flips to the Lindy."

"Would you chill!" said an irritable voice behind them. "Some people would like to watch without the commentary."

Lizzie turned around. "Gordo?" she asked in astonishment.

"Lizzie?" he replied.

"Quiet, all of you!" someone else said.

"Later," Lizzie whispered to Gordo, and they all settled down to watch the films.

Lizzie and Colin stood outside the Odeon, blinking in the late afternoon sun.

"So what did you think of Judy Garland and Mickey Rooney?" Colin asked.

"Well, the movie was kind of hokey," Lizzie admitted, "but it was fun. They both were ridiculously talented."

"Awesomely," Colin agreed.

It was also totally romantic. I kept watching Judy dance with Mickey and thinking, if only I could dance like that with Colin. . . .

"You want to go to the Digital Bean?" Colin asked. "I could use a latte."

Yes! There's only one little problem. . . .

"It's just that I'm wondering where my friend Gordo is," Lizzie said. "I haven't seen him come out yet."

"The guy who told me to shut up?" Colin asked, grinning.

"That's him," Lizzie admitted. "Gordo isn't usually cranky. And he was sitting all by himself. He doesn't usually go to movies alone."

At that moment Gordo emerged from the theater and walked straight up to them. "Lizzie," he said, "have you seen Lorene?"

"The girl you sat with in Alejandra's?" Lizzie guessed. Gordo nodded, and she gave him an apologetic shrug. "Sorry. I didn't know I was supposed to be looking for her. If she did come out of the theater, I missed her. What's up?"

"I was supposed to meet Lorene here, but I was late," Gordo explained. "Now I can't find her at all."

"Why don't you call her?" Colin suggested.

"I called her from the lobby," Gordo said glumly. "All I got was her voice mail."

Lizzie wasn't used to seeing Gordo so upset. He was always the sensible one, the one who kept it all in perspective when she and Miranda were wigging out. "Look," she said, "why don't you hang out with us? Colin and I are going to the Bean and—"

"Thanks, but no thanks," Gordo interrupted her. Before Lizzie could say another word, he turned and walked off.

Lizzie watched Gordo walk away from them, his shoulders slumped, his hands thrust into his pockets. He turned a corner and vanished from sight. Lizzie knew what she had to do. "I'm sorry," she told Colin. "But I need to make sure he's okay."

Even though I really want to go with you.

Lizzie didn't give Colin a chance to respond. She ran after Gordo, determined to catch up with him.

"What's going on?" she asked as they began to walk toward his house.

Gordo shook his head. "I told you that Lorene keeps asking me for advice about this Hypothetical Guy she likes. All along, it's sort of felt like it was me she was asking about."

"Your secret admirer," Lizzie said.

Gordo nodded, looking uncomfortable. "Well, last night she called for more guy advice, and then she asked me to meet her at this movie. And I thought, if she is my secret admirer, then it's a date. I was even getting up the courage to ask her after the movie—find out once and for all who this Hypothetical Guy is. And then the stupid bus broke down, and I was late and she thought I stood her up, and now it's all a mess!"

"Yikes," Lizzie said sympathetically. "But, Gordo, you don't really know that Lorene thinks you stood her up. You're just guessing that's what happened. I mean, maybe she got held up and never made it to the movie. There could be a whole other explanation."

"True," Gordo said, sounding a smidgen cheerier.

"You just need to call or e-mail and straighten out what really happened."

Gordo gave her a reluctant smile. "I thought I was the one who's supposed to give out all the sane advice."

Lizzie grinned. "I learned from a master."

Gordo looked at her curiously. "So who's Colin? It looked like you two were holding hands."

Lizzie blushed and gave Gordo the short version of the story, explaining how they had to dance together on Friday.

"You're going to dance onstage? In front of an audience?" Gordo stared at her in astonishment. "Have you, like, warned him of how you can barely walk down the hall without tripping over something?"

"Believe me," Lizzie said, "I tried."

Gordo shook his head. "Oh, man," he said softly. "Friday night is going to be extremely interesting."

Maybe it's not too late to flee to the Caribbean.

CHAPTER FIFTEEN

It was Sunday afternoon, and Lizzie was feel-ing bad.

Bad? I'm in the middle of a major, paralyzing guilt attack.

She felt awful about bailing on Colin after the movie, especially since it had felt like a date. She knew she ought to call and apologize. But what should she say? Maybe it hadn't bothered him. She picked up the phone—for the third time.

Isn't the third time supposed to be the charm? Just call already!

Lizzie forced herself to punch in the numbers. A woman's voice answered on the first ring. "Sandra Wolcott Dance Studio."

"Hi, this is Lizzie McGuire—"

"Lizzie, it's Sandra. I'm so glad you called."

"You are?" Lizzie hadn't expected such an enthusiastic response.

"What size are you, dear?" Sandra asked. "I need to order your costume."

Ulp! I'm really not going to get out of this, am I?

Lizzie gave her sizes for clothing and shoes, then she summoned her courage again. "Is Colin there?"

"No, he's at a friend's house."

"Well, will you tell him I called and—"

This was it. Lizzie knew she could just ask Sandra to tell Colin that she was sorry. But what if Sandra asked what she was sorry for? There was no way Lizzie was going to explain to Colin's mother that she had bailed on her son. It was all too embarrassing.

"Um, never mind," Lizzie said quickly. "I'll see him at the community center tomorrow and tell him myself."

"Are you sure?" Sandra asked kindly.

"Totally," Lizzie said, and hung up.

Gordo went into the *Chronicle* offices on Monday morning because he'd woken up to an e-mail from Jerome, asking him to come in. That had never happened before, and Gordo was curious.

Jerome's door was open. "Come in, David," he called.

Ingrid sat in a chair next to Jerome's desk. They seemed to be going over the typed pages she held in her hand. "I'd strengthen the ending," Jerome was telling her. "Play it out more, milk it for suspense. The rest is solid."

"Thanks," she told him.

Gordo tried not to do a double take. He recognized the typed pages. It was the story about the secret admirer that he found on the interns' computer.

Gordo's mind started to race. Did this mean that Ingrid was his secret admirer? If that was true, then who was Lorene's Hypothetical Guy?

Jerome's voice drew him out of his thoughts. "David, the reason I called you in is that I want to give you and Ingrid a special assignment. Kirkland Park is having its official dedication ceremony this morning. Since it was renovated with kids in mind—and since skateboarders will be performing—I'd like you two to cover it. It should be a cool event. How does that sound?"

"What time does the ceremony start?" Gordo asked, hoping he sounded like a pro. What he wanted to do was jump up and down with excitement. He and Ingrid were being sent on a real story, like real reporters! This was amazing!

"You've got a half hour to get over there,"

Jerome told them. "I suggest you leave now so you can get there ahead of time."

Gordo and Ingrid set off for the park at once. Gordo refused to take the bus, insisting they walk. "It's not that far," he told Ingrid, "and I don't trust buses."

"Yeah, well, you're not carrying twenty pounds of camera gear," Ingrid retorted.

Gordo sighed and offered to carry some gear, and Ingrid loaded him up with a tripod and one of her cameras.

They walked in silence for the first five minutes as Gordo tried to figure out a way to broach a delicate subject. Finally, he just came out with it. "You wrote the secret-admirer story that was on the computer in our office?"

"Yup." Ingrid didn't seem at all embarrassed by the question.

"Just for fun?" Gordo asked. "Or was there some other reason?"

"It was an over-the-summer English assignment," Ingrid explained. "I had to take one of my photos and write a story about it. The reason it was on the group computer is I brought it to the *Chronicle* offices to print out and show Jerome. Since he's an editor, I figured he could give me good writing advice."

"That makes sense," Gordo admitted. "Who was in the photo?"

Ingrid stopped walking and fished around in one of her bags. She pulled out a black-and-white glossy of a teenage boy and girl whom Gordo had never seen before. "I shot that at the amusement park," she said. "Something about the way she was looking at him seemed interesting and led to that story."

"That's pretty cool," Gordo said, handing back the photo. "I thought the story was too, by the way."

Ingrid sighed. "I should have known that if

I put it on that computer, everyone would read it."

"Sorry," Gordo said as they came to the park. He nodded at the crowds streaming by. "I bet they're going to our event."

They followed the crowds to the amphitheater, where rows of chairs faced the stage. Gordo grabbed a seat and took out his notebook and pen, while Ingrid set her camera on the tripod.

The mayor came to the front of the stage and gave an introduction, then one politician after another got up and made speeches. Each one, it seemed, took credit for Kirkland's renovation and then thanked everybody in the phone book for helping them.

Two hours later the mayor called for a break, promising "more festivities to come."

"I'm not sure I can take any more," Gordo told Ingrid. He looked down at his notebook and shook his head. "I stopped taking notes six speakers ago."

"None of them said anything, anyway," Ingrid assured him. "I stopped taking pictures, too."

The mayor took the stage again.

Suddenly, Matt McGuire zoomed across the stage on a skateboard, in front of an astonished mayor. Lanny was standing on the edge of the stage, where he was putting vinyl disks on two turntables.

Matt brought the board to a stop right in front of the turntables. He removed his helmet, took his place behind the turntables, and began to scratch and mix and sing about skateboarding while Lanny shook a tambourine.

Within seconds, the audience was up on its feet, dancing and chanting the chorus. Startled, the mayor stepped back from the mike as two skateboarders crossed the stage on their boards. Gordo began to scribble furiously. *This* was the story.

Lizzie had an awful feeling right in the center of her chest. It was because she'd been at the senior center all day, and she still hadn't explained things to Colin.

He hadn't said much to her during rehearsal that morning. He had probably been waiting for her to say something.

Lizzie knew she should have apologized. It had just seemed too embarrassing to talk about on a stage filled with seniors. Plus, even though last Saturday it had felt like a totally romantic date to her, she didn't know if he'd felt the same way. Now it was almost four o'clock. If she hurried, she could catch him before he left the auditorium for the day.

She told Ada she had to leave early and headed toward the main building. She wasn't even halfway there, when she saw Ethan Craft coming toward her.

"Yo, Lizzie," he said. "I've been looking all over for you. We need to talk."

Lizzie was instantly on cloud nine.

Ethan's been looking for me! He wants to talk! And best of all, he used the pronoun *we*!

"What's up?" Lizzie asked as casually as she could.

"My stepmom is looking for a babysitter for my little sister. I told her I'd ask around. Do you babysit?"

Okay, the only person I ever babysat for was Matt. And it turned into kind of a disaster, but it was totally *not* my fault!

"Of course I babysit," Lizzie answered.

"Cool," Ethan said. "Does that mean you're interested in applying for the job?"

A job in crush-boy's house!? Is this for real?

"Sure," Lizzie said, "I guess I'm interested."

"Great. Then my stepmother wants you to fill this out." Ethan handed her a manila envelope. Lizzie drew out a five-page form and began to read aloud.

"'One. Describe your babysitting experience. Please provide references from least five families. Two,'" Lizzie continued. "'Describe the steps you would take to handle each of the following emergencies: flood, fire, earthquake, and snakebite.'"

What about elephant stampedes? I'm amazing when it comes to dealing with elephant stampedes.

Lizzie looked up at Ethan. "Snakebite in Hillridge? Is she serious?"

"You have no idea," Ethan said solemnly.

Lizzie continued to read. Mrs. Craft wanted her to describe first-aid procedures, suitable songs and activities, and a list of books she would and would not read to kids. And that was only the first page.

Lizzie sighed and returned the form to the envelope. "I'm really sorry, Ethan," she said. "But I don't think I'm qualified to work for your stepmother."

CHAPTER SIXTEEN

On Wednesday morning Lizzie woke up to an e-mail from Miranda. The message read: You have to come to Alejandra's on Friday at 4:30. Don't ask why. Just be there!

Now what is she up to?

Then she thought about Colin. She still hadn't told him what a great time she'd had or apologized for leaving so abruptly. But she'd see him today and make things right.

One hour later, Lizzie entered the seniors' lounge. The six seniors who were dancing swing were all in costume. The men wore loose, black pants and white shirts with brightly colored suspenders. The women wore full, calf-length skirts, and button-down blouses, their colors matching the men's suspenders. "You guys look hot!" Lizzie said.

"We are hot," Marcus agreed. "I keep telling Ada she's got to adjust the air-conditioning in this room."

"Lizzie!" Sandra came over to her, a garment bag draped over one arm. "I have your costume here. You're going to love it."

"Really?" Lizzie asked.

"Try it on and see what you think," Sandra said. "You can use the studio."

Lizzie took the garment bag to the room lined with mirrors. She pulled out a fitted, petal-pink button-down blouse and a short, full skirt. The skirt was a deeper shade of pink, more of a dusky rose. At the bottom of the bag were pink bobby socks and black-and-white saddle shoes. Lizzie put it all on, studied her reflection, and laughed. She felt as if she'd just stepped out of the musical *Grease*, but she had to admit, the costume was totally adorable.

"Very smart!" Harriet said with a smile as Lizzie returned to the lounge.

"You look positively ducky!" Clarice added.

"It's perfect!" Sandra said. "Now everyone to the auditorium for our dress rehearsal."

"Dress rehearsal?" Lizzie asked weakly.

"You'll be fine, don't worry," Sandra said. "Come on, let's get to the auditorium. Colin's waiting."

Lizzie, with dread thick in her heart, filed into the auditorium with the others.

"Places, please!" Sandra called.

Colin, she saw, was dressed like the men, in the white shirt and loose, black pants. His suspenders were a steel blue that matched the rims on his glasses. Lizzie looked at him in surprise. On the senior men, the costumes looked like cool, but comfortable, clothing. But on Colin's lean frame the loose, flowing costume looked . . . completely amazing, almost like he'd stepped out of the pages of a fashion magazine.

Lizzie got up on the stage, while Sandra called up the music on the laptop. Lizzie took a deep breath and went right up to Colin. "I'm really sorry about Saturday," she said. "I didn't mean to bolt on you."

"Forget it," Colin said nonchalantly. "Let's just rehearse."

Maybe I was just imagining things. Maybe the movie wasn't a date, after all. Or did I totally mess things up?

The intro to the first dance began to play. Like the others, Lizzie began tapping her feet as Sandra called, "And five, six, seven, eight."

"Triple step, triple step," Lizzie murmured while trying to follow Colin's lead. She triple-stepped right on top of his toe. Colin winced and said, "Just try it again."

"Lizzie, don't forget to bend your knees," Sandra called. "You look a little stiff."

"Right," Lizzie murmured, concentrating on bending her knees.

"And turn!" Sandra called.

Lizzie, seeing that she was at least two steps behind everyone else, turned in a rush—and clipped Colin on the jaw with her elbow.

Now he's never going to like me.

Lizzie stopped, appalled. "Are you all right?" she asked. "I'm so sorry!"

Colin rubbed his jaw. "I'll survive," he said. "Come on, keep dancing and try to remember to keep your elbows in on the turns."

"Right, elbows in," Lizzie murmured, concentrating even harder.

I don't even concentrate this hard when I'm studying for a test.

The dress rehearsal didn't improve. Lizzie lost her place several times, was behind the beat almost all the time, and kept turning away from Colin when she was supposed to turn toward him. At one point, she caught Sandra shaking her head with dismay.

Still, at the end of the rehearsal Sandra managed to be upbeat. "Don't worry, everyone," she said. "There's an old theater superstition: bad dress rehearsal, great performance! So it's going to be fine. Just try to relax and work on your steps."

Lizzie shot Colin a panicked look. "But I still don't know the steps."

"I've got dress rehearsals for the other performers this morning," he said. "But why don't we rehearse at my mom's studio tomorrow, okay?"

"I guess," Lizzie agreed.

Ada was fine with Lizzie using the afternoon to rehearse. "Of course," she said. "At least that boy is worth your time."

"What do you mean by that?" Lizzie asked in frustration.

"I'm sure you know," Ada said mysteriously, and went to help someone in the drumming group adjust her costume.

Jasmine, who'd been standing nearby, raised one dark eyebrow. "It might sound crazy, but you probably ought to listen to her," she told Lizzie.

"Why? What makes Ada such an expert on my life?" Lizzie asked.

Jasmine started laughing. "Don't you know who Ada was before she retired and started doing this job?"

Lizzie shook her head.

"She was Ask Ada, the advice columnist. She was in, like, hundreds of newspapers every day."

"That is very bizarre," Lizzie said.

"But true. Haven't you noticed how smart she is about people and making things work around here?"

"Huh," Lizzie said. Maybe Ada was right. Maybe Colin had been the one for her all along.

Gordo left his editorial meeting, baffled. It

was Wednesday, and Lorene hadn't been in all week. It was almost like she disappeared last weekend. He'd tried calling, and just got her answering machine. He'd tried e-mailing and got no response at all.

He was so caught up in his thoughts about Lorene that he didn't see Ingrid coming out of the darkroom. They collided, and Ingrid's big canvas bag fell to the floor.

"Sorry," Gordo said. He bent over to pick it up and recognized the magazine that had half slid out. "This is your *Fashion Forward*?" he asked.

"Yep."

"Seriously?" Gordo couldn't believe it.

Ingrid picked up the magazine and opened it to the hottie article. "I was studying this article for the photographs."

For the first time, Gordo noticed that the two-page spread was illustrated with about a dozen photos of guys and girls.

"See, they're all in these typical, dopey teen-magazine poses," Ingrid explained. "He's kind of slouching against a wall, she's got her chin on her hand, he's sitting on the hood of a car, arms crossed over his chest. . . . I would never in a million years pose people like that, except I'm pretty sure it's what Queen Kate wants, and so far I haven't been able to give her anything that makes her happy."

Gordo grinned at her. "I didn't think you cared about making Kate happy."

Ingrid grinned back. "Personally, I'd get great satisfaction out of making her as miserable as she makes everyone else. But as far as photography goes—if I'm going to make it as a pro, I've got to be able to take pictures that will please any editor. So I was trying to figure out what Kate wants and how I can do it."

"So the short story and the magazine were

yours," Gordo said slowly. "How about the symbolic bouquet that was left in the interns' office—the one from the secret admirer?"

Ingrid laughed. "You think I would have left that for you? No offense," she said quickly. "I didn't even know there was a bouquet."

Gordo felt like an idiot. How could he have admitted out loud that he thought he had a secret admirer? And could anyone be less interested in him than Ingrid was?

"Listen," she said. "I think you're a good person and a really good reporter, but what I've been concentrating on all summer is work." Now she was the one who looked a little embarrassed. "Everyone says I'm way too serious. I guess they're right."

"No," Gordo said. "You're absolutely fine the way you are. I just got caught up in—" He couldn't even finish the sentence.

"I thought your article on the park

dedication was really good," she said, chang-
ing the subject.

"Thanks," Gordo said appreciatively.

"Hey, Ingrid," he said as she started out of
the office. "Just for the record, I'm really glad
we got to work together this summer."

"Same here," she said.

CHAPTER SEVENTEEN

Lizzie took a last glance in the mirror before grabbing the bag containing her saddle shoes. She was wearing jeans, her flip-flops, and an embroidered peasant blouse. She figured it was an okay outfit for practicing at Sandra's studio with Colin on a Thursday afternoon. Her stomach still hurt when she thought of actually dancing onstage, but she was looking forward to this practice session.

Downstairs in the kitchen, she found Matt

and Lanny stuffing their McGuire M & E posters in the trash. Was the little weirdo actually giving up on one of his terrible ideas? It was too good to be true.

"What are you doing?" Lizzie asked, dying of curiosity.

"Change of career," Matt announced.

Why do I have a bad feeling?

Lizzie phrased her question warily. "You're giving up music?"

"Not hardly. The mayor realized that Lanny and I got all the attention at his park dedication ceremony. So he hired us."

Lizzie couldn't believe it. "To do what? Scare off his opponents?"

"He's got a bunch of public speeches to give this summer," Matt explained. "So he's hired me and Lanny to open for him, to sort of set the tone, get everyone all enthusiastic. It's an exclusive gig. Lanny negotiated it." Lanny took a little bow at these words. "We are now officially known as His Honor's Hot New Hits." He smirked at her.

"That's just typical," Lizzie muttered as she headed out the door. "One hundred percent typical!"

Twenty minutes later, Lizzie arrived at Sandra's dance studio. She saw Colin through the door. "Here goes nothing," she said to herself.

Colin, who was wearing jeans and a faded T-shirt, held out his hands to her.

Lizzie walked toward him, then came to a stop, suddenly overwhelmed. "Colin, it's no good," she said. "The rehearsal was awful. And tomorrow night's the performance. It's going to be just as bad. You've got to ask your mom to go back to using just three couples."

Colin's brown eyes studied her for a moment, then he turned off the music. "Asking you to learn three dances in a week when you've never done any partner dancing at all is huge," he admitted.

"Exactly," Lizzie said. "There's no way I can memorize three dances' worth of steps.

And don't forget, I'm a klutz!

"So maybe it's not such a good idea," she

went on in a small voice. "Maybe we should just forget about it."

"You know," Colin said thoughtfully, "after the rehearsal, I realized that you're concentrating on individual steps when what you need to learn is patterns."

Did he not hear anything I just said?

"Look," Colin said, "let's just practice this afternoon. If you don't feel better afterward, I promise I'll talk to my mom. Fair enough?"

Lizzie nodded. She couldn't exactly disagree when he was being so reasonable. Plus, he didn't seem mad at her about the whole movie thing. He was being really nice.

"First pattern," Colin said, "triple-step, triple-step, rock-step, turn. First, say it aloud a few times."

Lizzie chanted the pattern, feeling more than a little silly.

"Now try doing the steps by yourself," he said. "I'll watch."

I'd rather have you watch me floss my teeth.

"No way," Lizzie said flatly. "That's too embarrassing."

Colin rolled his eyes. "Okay, I'll dance it for you first, then we'll dance it facing the mirror, then you try."

Lizzie reluctantly agreed, and though she

still felt about as graceful as a waddling turkey, she managed to perform the pattern. Colin nodded encouragingly and gave her the next set of steps. She managed to get through those as well, and then they danced both patterns together.

The first dance ended with Lizzie doing a spin into Colin's arms. She stood there a moment. She was leaning back against him, and he had one arm around her waist. She felt perfectly comfortable, as if it were exactly where she belonged.

"Nice," Colin said softly, and released her.

They worked on a third and fourth pattern and then a fifth, and before Lizzie knew it, they had gotten through two of the three dances. She wasn't exactly smooth, but she had a much better idea of what she was supposed to be doing. And she genuinely liked dancing with Colin.

"Should we do the third one?" Lizzie asked a little breathlessly.

"I wish we could," he said, "but there's a class starting in ten minutes." He nodded toward the window, and Lizzie saw a tall, very beautiful girl coming toward the studio. "Listen," he went on, "write down your e-mail address, and I'll write out the patterns and send them to you tonight."

Lizzie gave him her e-mail address, then sat down on the floor, removed her saddle shoes, and stuffed them into her bag.

The door opened and the girl came in.

Lizzie got to her feet. The girl was even more beautiful up close. She looked to be about their age and had long, black waist-length hair that was held back by two silver clips. She wore a short wraparound dancer's skirt, and her legs were longer and even more perfect than Kate's.

"Colin, I've missed you!" she cried, then she threw her arms around him and hugged him tight.

Colin hugged Beautiful Girl back, while Lizzie mumbled something and left quickly.

Lizzie had gotten about two blocks away from the studio before she realized that she'd left her purse and the bag with her saddle shoes on the studio floor.

Lizzie sighed. She could probably ask Colin to bring the saddle shoes to the community center tomorrow. But her purse? It had her wallet with money for the bus home. I could walk, Lizzie decided. Until she realized what else was in her purse: her favorite lip gloss, blush, and mascara.

There's no way I can survive without them.

Knowing she had no choice, Lizzie turned and walked back to the dance studio.

Big band music was playing when Lizzie opened the studio door. Colin and Beautiful Girl were doing the most incredible dancing Lizzie had ever seen. They looked as if they were gliding across the floor. They moved together in perfect sync as Colin spun her— three tight, perfect turns in a row—and swung her so that she took off in gorgeous aerial moves, high over his head. She landed gracefully, and they moved into a series of fast precise steps.

The dance ended with Colin dipping her so that she leaned back against his arm, back arched, head nearly touching the floor, and one leg straight up in the air. Then Colin helped her up and they hugged again.

Lizzie watched it all openmouthed. She knew Colin was a good dancer, but she had never realized that he was this amazing.

Can he be this incredible and still like someone who can barely get through one basic dance? Uh, negative.

She knew then that Beautiful Girl was his perfect match. Why had she ever thought Colin liked her?

"Lizzie, hi." Colin noticed her standing there and smiled. "You came back."

Lizzie swallowed hard and darted forward to retrieve her shoes and purse. "Forgot these," she said, trying to smile. Before Colin could respond, she fled from the dance studio.

CHAPTER EIGHTEEN

On Friday afternoon, Lizzie arrived at Alejandra's at four thirty. She found Miranda standing behind the taco bar.

"Where is everyone?" Lizzie asked.

"My aunt is running an errand, Hector dashed out for some CD he had to have, and the evening waiters haven't come on yet," Miranda reported. "Luckily, we don't have any customers at the moment. Let me make you a smoothie. What flavor do you want?"

Lizzie chose a tropical fruit mix, and Miranda got the blender whirring.

"So, why did you ask me to come here today?" Lizzie asked as she sipped the delicious icy drink.

"I haven't seen you all week. I missed you," Miranda answered.

At that moment, the front door opened and Josh walked in. "*Holá*," Miranda called to him.

"Hey," Josh said, looking happy to see her. He nodded at Lizzie and glanced around. "It's awfully quiet here today."

Miranda looked at the clock above the taco bar. "You don't have to start for another fifteen minutes," she told him. "Why don't you sit down and have a smoothie?"

Josh looked hesitant, then sat down and ordered a kiwi-raspberry concoction. He and Lizzie glanced at each other quickly, then looked away. Lizzie realized that once again they didn't really have anything to say to each other, but this time she didn't care. Josh was cute, but she knew they weren't right for each other. They just hadn't clicked.

Miranda slid Josh's drink toward him. "Josh, did you tell Lizzie about that skateboard contest you won?"

"Uh, no, I didn't," Josh said.

Miranda looked at Lizzie imploringly. "Did you tell him about the seniors' drumming group at the center?"

"Why would I?" Lizzie asked. Then she remembered his grandmother and thought maybe that was what Miranda was getting at. "Uh, Josh," Lizzie said. "Does your grandmother play drums?"

Josh rolled his eyes. "That's like asking if my grandmother plays wide receiver for the Packers."

Lizzie started to get indignant. "It wasn't ridiculous to ask if your grandmother plays drums," she said. "We have a drumming group at the senior center."

"I thought I already made it clear that the center and my grandmother are not a good mix," Josh said firmly.

"That was just a freak accident with the cat," Lizzie retorted.

Josh shook his head. "Just forget it."

"Fine," Lizzie said. And to her surprise Lizzie realized it *was* fine. It didn't matter what Josh thought of her. Colin was what mattered to her, even if he was obviously in love with Beautiful Girl.

The restaurant phone rang then. "I'll get that," Miranda said. "You two talk."

Josh looked from Miranda to Lizzie, then got up. "Sorry, I've got work to do," he said.

I think it's officially time for Miranda to drop the matchmaking.

Miranda picked up the ringing phone. "Alejandra's," she said, "could you please hold?" She didn't even give the caller a chance to answer. She pushed down the HOLD button and took off after Josh, who was crossing the courtyard, on his way to the kitchen.

"Josh, how could you be so rude?" Miranda demanded. "What is your problem?"

Josh whirled on her. "You want to know what the problem is? *You're* the problem. You have got to be the densest person on earth!"

Miranda stared at him in confusion. "Me? What are you talking about? All I want to know is why you were so mean to Lizzie!"

Josh looked so angry she could almost see steam coming out of his ears. "Maybe I'm just tired of Lizzie and you and this whole restaurant!" he cried.

Miranda heard her aunt's voice behind them. "You don't want to work in the restaurant anymore? If that's the case, I think it's best if I give you your paycheck now."

"You're firing me?" Josh asked in disbelief.

"I am," Alejandra said.

"*Tia*, you're not being fair," Miranda protested.

"Maybe not," her aunt said, "but I have a business to run, and that means we all work together smoothly. Anything else, I don't have time for."

"Great," Josh said angrily. "I'll leave you to your smooth business."

Without even waiting for his check, he stormed out of the restaurant.

Moments later, Lizzie found Miranda in the courtyard, blinking back tears. "What happened?" Lizzie asked. "You look like you've been crying."

"Josh got angry at me, and my aunt fired him," Miranda said bleakly. "All I was trying to do was get you two together, and everything went wrong."

"Miranda, don't you see?" Lizzie said. "The reason Josh was so upset is because *you're* the one he's been crushing on! And you kept pushing him at me."

"But you saw him first," Miranda said.

"That's superloyal of you, and I appreciate it, but it doesn't make me and Josh right for each other. The truth is, I'm not even interested in Josh anymore."

"You're not?" Miranda asked.

"Lately, the boy I can't stop thinking about is Colin Lang," Lizzie confessed.

"Really?" Miranda asked. "I thought he was really moody."

"It turned out he was just really stressed about his job and then annoyed when his mom made him dance. But he's really sweet, and dancing with him is so . . . amazing. But once tonight's performance is over, he probably won't even look at me again. He's already met his perfect match. I saw them together."

"Are you sure?" Miranda asked.

Am I sure? All she was missing was a neon sign that flashed: I'M COLIN'S PERFECT MATCH!

Lizzie nodded.

"That's harsh," Miranda said.

"Do you like Josh?" Lizzie asked her friend.

"A lot," Miranda admitted. "We get along really well. But I didn't say anything because I knew you liked him."

"I'm sorry," Lizzie said. "I should have realized sooner that Josh and I aren't right for each other. But you and Josh are. You should tell him how you feel."

Miranda smiled at her best friend. "Okay, I will. Thanks, Lizzie."

At least Miranda's still got a chance with the boy she likes. Sigh.

* * *

Gordo finished putting in changes on his latest article and hit the PRINT button on the interns' computer. It was nearly five o'clock and the *Chronicle* offices were quiet. It seemed that in the summer, everyone left early on Fridays.

He removed the pages from the printer and was standing there, reading them over, when Lorene raced in.

"Oh, Gordo, I'm so glad you're still here." She stood beaming at him for moment, then threw her arms around him, murmuring, "You're the best!"

"I am?" Gordo asked. Even if Lorene *was* his mysterious admirer, this was too weird. Gordo untangled her arms from around his neck and stepped back. "Uh, what exactly did I do?"

"I'll show you!" she said. "But you have to come outside with me. Right now!"

"O-kay," Gordo agreed. He was getting ready to leave, anyway. He put his papers in his book bag, shut down the computer, and followed her out of the newspaper offices.

"Wait a minute," Gordo said. "Where have you been all week?"

Lorene looked sheepish. "Home with the flu. I'm sorry I didn't answer your e-mails, but it was hard to sit at the computer when I felt so lousy. But now everything's better!"

As they stepped into the elevator Gordo tried for a cool 'tude, but his heart was jumping around like he had a trampoline inside his chest. Maybe Lorene was going to admit that she had left him the bouquet, that he was Hypothetical Guy. He wasn't sure if he was thrilled or terrified.

Lorene hooked her arm through his as the elevator reached the ground floor. "Oh, Gordo, I don't know what I would have done without all your advice. You were, like, such a big help."

"I was?" Gordo asked.

"Absolutely. I mean, there were so many times I almost ruined everything—like that day I left the symbolic bouquet in the office by mistake."

"You left it there by mistake?" Gordo repeated. He tried to make sense of this. If it was a mistake, that meant Lorene hadn't left it for him. That meant he didn't have a secret admirer, after all. Gordo's heart stopped its acrobatic leaping around and settled into a sad little bog of depression.

Lorene was still holding his arm as they left the building. She escorted him over to a slightly pudgy guy waiting by the fountain.

"Gordo, this is Tom. Tom and I are in a theater group," she explained.

Lorene had been telling the truth, Gordo realized. All along, Lorene had been crushing on Tom.

Gordo studied Hypothetical Guy. Tom

wasn't what Lizzie or Miranda would call hot or even cute, but there was something in his expression that made Gordo think he had a good sense of humor.

"Hi," Gordo said.

"Hi." Tom stuck out his hand. "Lorene says you're one of her best friends."

Gordo thought that over as they shook hands. What had actually gone on between him and Lorene was a lot like the way things were with him and Lizzie and Miranda. "Yeah," he said. "It's been great working together on the paper."

Gordo really wanted to get out of there. But he also needed to prove to himself that he could handle this. "What are you guys doing tonight?" he asked.

"No plans yet," Lorene admitted.

"Well, then how about going to Talent Night at the HCC? The senior center is putting it on, and my friend Lizzie says there are going to be some unforgettable acts."

"That sounds cool," Tom said.

"Are you going to be there?" Lorene asked.

"Wouldn't miss it," Gordo said.

"Then I'll bring my cousin Tamsin," Lorene promised. "For a while now I've been thinking that you two would be perfect for each other."

Miranda was alone in the taco area, wiping off one of the tables. She glanced up at the clock. It wasn't even six. Everything seemed to be in slow motion since the fight with Josh. So she couldn't quite believe it when she saw him coming toward her across the courtyard.

"Where did you come from?" she asked.

"The kitchen," he said. "I went in the back way. I wanted to apologize to your aunt for losing my temper—and to you."

"I owe you an apology, too," Miranda said, her voice unsteady. "I shouldn't have tried to push you and Lizzie together."

"No argument there," Josh said with a sigh. "Why did you?"

"Because she's my best friend and she liked you the first time she saw you." Miranda bit back a smile. "But now she's totally crushing on someone else."

"What about you?" Josh asked.

"I liked you, too," Miranda admitted. "A lot."

Josh hesitated a moment, suddenly seeming shy. "And the situation now?"

"I still like you," Miranda said. "But you haven't said how you feel!" she added indignantly.

"I thought it was totally obvious that I've been crushing on you since that block party. I mean, *you're* the reason I've been willing to spend another summer washing dishes!"

"I am?" Miranda asked.

"Yeah, you are. I sat by you at the movie and danced with you at the park. I always linger after my shift to spend more time with you." Josh stepped toward her, smiling. "Your aunt just offered me my job back. How would you feel if I took her up on it?"

Miranda returned his smile. "I'd feel fine about that," she said. "Perfectly fine!"

Josh stepped closer to Miranda. He leaned in and kissed her.

Just then, Alejandra stepped into the courtyard and cleared her throat. Josh and Miranda moved apart, embarrassed.

"I could use some help moving a table, Josh," Alejandra said.

"Sure," Josh said, and stole a glance at Miranda as he went to help.

She smiled at him. The kiss had been amazing.

CHAPTER NINETEEN

"How are you feeling?" Colin asked Lizzie.

Lizzie glanced in the backstage mirror and made a slight adjustment to her costume. "Nervous," she admitted. "All day long I've been reciting dance patterns in my head. That e-mail you sent last night was great, but I feel like I've been cramming for an exam."

Colin touched her shoulder lightly. "It's going to be a lot more fun than that, I promise. I bet you'll remember more than you think.

You've been doing well in our practices."

"But I feel like a poser," Lizzie said truthfully. "I'm not a dancer."

"Neither is anyone else here," Colin reminded her. "Clarice and Marcus and the others, none of them are pros."

"You are," Lizzie said.

"Not really. I was never at a professional level. I was just an amateur with a lot of training and a pushy mom. And now," he said, giving her an apologetic look, "I've got to go help my dad set things up."

"Your father?" Lizzie asked, surprised.

Colin grinned. "Someone's got to do the tech work while we're dancing."

Lizzie tried not to fidget too much as she listened to Ada welcome the audience. Thinking about the actual performance made her nervous.

Instead, her thoughts went to Colin.

How totally unfair is it that just when I realized I liked Colin, he turned out to be crushing on someone else!

She felt a gentle touch on her shoulder. "It's going to be all right, dear," Clarice said. "You'll see. Everything will work out."

Sandra came toward them. "You two should be waiting with the others," she said. "We're onstage in two minutes."

Lizzie couldn't resist taking a sneak peek at the audience. All the teens who volunteered at the HCC were there, including Jasmine and a boy who had to be Zeke. Ethan sat with the evil Kate, but for once Lizzie didn't care. Josh and his grandmother were there, sitting beside Miranda and Rosa. And the other interns from the *Chronicle* were in one row— Tudge, Lorene and a date, Ingrid, and Gordo, who was with a pretty girl whom Lizzie didn't recognize. Sitting right up front was the McGuire contingent—Lizzie's parents and the little reptile.

Ulp! Is it too late for that trip to the Caribbean?

Then Colin was at her side, taking her hand. "Come on," he said gently. "We need to go over here."

She followed him to a spot in the wings behind Clarice and Marcus. Lizzie heard the applause signaling the end of Ada's speech. Then she and the other dancers took their places onstage.

The music started and the curtain rose. Lizzie stood absolutely still, a cold blanket of fear wrapping itself around her and freezing her in place.

"Lizzie?" Colin whispered. He gave her hand a slight squeeze.

"I'm—I'm scared," she murmured.

Make that terrified.

"I know," Colin said, "but you're going to be fantastic. Five, six, seven, eight . . . triple-step, triple-step . . ."

And they were dancing. Lizzie's mind went blank. She couldn't remember the patterns or the steps. Somehow, though, her body seemed to remember. She was moving stiffly but doing all the right steps. She kept her knees bent, her elbows in, and managed to turn in the right direction. At least for the first song.

The second song began and Colin pulled her close. Wow, this is nice, Lizzie thought.

"You're doing great," he said. "Just try to loosen up a little. Ease into the music."

Lizzie tried. She concentrated on feeling the beat, and her muscles relaxed. But she gave an enthusiastic kick, and her left saddle shoe went flying across the stage. The audience howled.

Mortified, Lizzie started to go after the shoe, but Colin pulled her back. "It's okay," he told her. "Just go with it. The audience loved it."

It was true, she realized. The audience had started clapping in time to the music. And the foot with only the sock did a great slide.

Colin spun Lizzie into a turn, and she did an extra turn, got a little dizzy, but then found her way back into the music, following Colin across the stage.

It was over as suddenly as it had begun. They bowed to the audience—Lizzie managed a curtsy—and Colin was leading her into the wings. After what sounded like deafening applause, the entire swing group returned to the stage for a second curtain call.

I survived the performance, one shoe and all. Too bad I totally embarrassed Colin.

* * *

"Where's Precious tonight?" Lizzie asked Josh's grandmother. The talent show was over, and she was mingling with the audience.

"I found a dogsitter," Mrs. Russell announced proudly.

Now she finds a dogsitter!

"You know, I've always loved watching the Lindy Hop," Mrs. Russell went on. "I couldn't bear to miss this."

"Do you like to dance?" Lizzie asked her. "Because I'm sure that Sandra will keep teaching the swing classes."

"Well, perhaps I could hire the dogsitter more often," Mrs. Russell said. "I just might have to give the senior center another try."

Lizzie looked around. Miranda, who was standing next to Josh and holding his hand, mouthed a "thank you!" to her. Lizzie gave her a thumbs-up. And Gordo seemed to be very interested in a girl who looked a lot like him. She was skinny, with curly brown hair—only she was cuter than Gordo, and her clothes were totally stylin'.

Finally, Lizzie's eyes were drawn to Colin, who stood talking with his mom and a man who looked like an older version of Colin. It had to be his dad.

Lizzie knew that she had to let go of her feelings for Colin. She was sure she had humiliated him with her clown dancing.

Not to mention, he's got Beautiful Girl.

"Lizzie." Her mom gave her a hug. "You were wonderful!"

"No, I wasn't," Lizzie said honestly.

"You were," Mrs. McGuire insisted. "You made a few mistakes, but overall you danced beautifully. And the audience loved you!"

Sometimes my mom really gets me. And sometimes she doesn't. At all.

"I'm kind of tired," Lizzie said. "Could we go home now?"

"Your father's talking to Harriet," her mother said. "I think she's trying to recruit him for a power walk."

Someone touched Lizzie's wrist. It was Colin. "Lizzie, could I talk to you for a minute?"

"Go ahead," Mrs. McGuire said. "I have to find your brother, anyway."

"It's too noisy here," Colin said. "Let's go backstage."

Lizzie followed him, feeling queasy with nerves. She couldn't imagine why he wanted to talk with her.

Unless it's to tell me what a bad job I did.

Backstage, the auditorium noise was muffled by the thick stage curtain.

Colin sat down on one of the big, black prop boxes. "So, we did great," he said.

"You did great," Lizzie corrected him. "I was terrible."

"That's not true—"

"Stop trying to make me feel good!" Lizzie said. "I know you've had better dance partners than me."

Colin shrugged. "Technically speaking, yes. But—"

"I saw you dancing with her," Lizzie blurted out, unable to stop herself. "The girl with the long, black hair. And I understand that she's the one you want. I mean, it's totally understandable. She's your perfect match."

Colin sat up straight. "Are you talking about Desiree? The girl I was dancing with when you came back for your bag?"

Lizzie nodded miserably.

"Lizzie, listen to me," Colin said. "Desiree was my dance partner. We started dancing together when I was eight. We competed until the end of last year, when I stopped dancing."

"Did you win a lot?" Lizzie asked.

Colin nodded. "Yeah, we did. And she's still winning with her new partner. The thing you need to know is, she and I have never been romantic about each other."

"Never?" Lizzie couldn't believe it.

"She's two years older than me. And she's got a boyfriend she's crazy about. Des and I—we've been through a lot together, but we're just friends."

"And you like dancing with her?"

"I like dancing," Colin said firmly. "What I don't like are the competitions."

"But you're used to being really good. Just now, in the performance, didn't I embarrass you? To death?"

Colin reached for Lizzie's hand and drew her down so that she was sitting beside him.

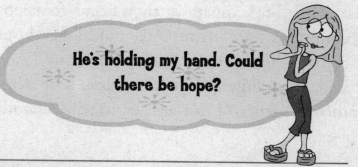

He's holding my hand. Could there be hope?

"No," he said, and looked into her eyes. "That was the first time I performed and actually enjoyed it. For once, I was able to forget about doing everything perfectly. All I wanted was to have fun with you." He was still holding her hand in his. "You're a lot of fun, Lizzie McGuire."

He leaned toward her then, and kissed her. All Lizzie's nervousness and doubts melted away, and in their place she felt the excitement of something new and wonderful.

"I've been wanting to do that for a long time now," Colin admitted. "I just couldn't tell if you liked me."

"I do," Lizzie said. She kissed him again.

They broke apart as they heard footsteps coming toward them. Ada poked her head through the curtain. "There you are," she said, sounding not at all surprised to find them together. "I just wanted to tell you both that you were splendid. Your performance brought down the house! And that bit with the shoe—did you plan it that way?"

"Not exactly," Lizzie admitted. "I actually meant to get it all right."

Ada gave Lizzie one of her shrewd looks. "Oh, I think you got it right this time. Have a good evening, you two."

One week later, Lizzie left the senior center in a totally cheerful mood. It was the end of the week, and she was on her way to meet Colin at the dance studio for a swing lesson. As she crossed the lawn of the community center, she saw Miranda on one of the benches.

"What are you doing here?" Lizzie asked.

"Waiting for you," Miranda said. "I wanted you to be the first one to hear the awesome news. Josh invited me to go to a baseball game with him on Sunday!"

Lizzie grinned. "The date part is good. But baseball, the most boring sport ever? I still don't know how anyone gets through a game without falling asleep."

"Oh, I'll be wide awake," Miranda said confidently. "Hey, did you hear? Gordo and Tamsin are going out, sort of."

"What does that mean?" Lizzie wondered.

"It's classic Gordo," Miranda explained. "He and Tamsin aren't going to do anything as clichéd as dating. Instead, they're going to make a video together, documenting unusual starts to romantic relationships."

Lizzie smiled. "Like getting drafted into dancing in a talent show for senior citizens?"

"Or falling for the boy you're trying to set up with your best friend?" Miranda suggested with a giggle.

"Or for the man you find completely annoying?" added Clarice. She was walking by them, her arm linked through Marcus's. She gave Lizzie a sly wink. "Didn't I tell you it would all work out, dear? It's a totally hottie summer."

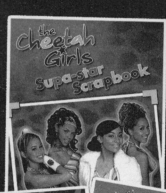

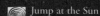